Polypetalous

Elliana Leigh

First Printing: 2024
Alanna Rusnak Publishing

Library and Archives Canada Cataloguing in Publication
CIP data on file with the National Library and Archives

ISBN trade paperback edition: 978-1-990336-78-2
ISBN hardcover edition: 978-1-990336-79-9

Alanna Rusnak Publishing is an imprint of Chicken House Press

282906 Normanby/Bentinck Townline
Durham, Ontario, Canada, N0G 1R0
www.chickenhousepress.ca

to Mrs. Emily Miller for introducing me to the world of writing
and to my Mom for supporting me in my endeavors.

Table of Contents

vii   Acknowledgements

ix   About the Author

xi   Foreword

1.   Playground Fear

5.   Memories

15.   Crow

19.   The Consequences of War

31.   The Tunnel

35.   Grim Reaper

39.   The Forgotten Knight

45.   The Dance of the Flowers

49.   1966

55.   Pepper Dragon

63.   Traitors

67.   Car Crash

71.   Orange Ribbon

97.   Banished

101. The Oregon Trail

107. Homeless

113. Cats and Colors

115. Heirloom

119. Cage

125. Nightmare

131. Hospital

135. Agramus

139. Dream

147. Mist

151. Bonus Story

Acknowledgements

To Alanna, my editor and publisher, for her dedication and encouragement.

To Kali Morse for helping improve my stories, and to Diana Reynolds for helping me polish them.

To my reading and writing teachers, Emily Miller, Meagan Davis, Dorthy Schroeder, and Terri Clarke for teaching me about story structure and how to write an intriguing plot. :)

To my Mom for supporting and loving me, thank you for helping me with my art and writing.

To my Dad, the funniest man alive, thank you for raising me to be myself.

To my Brother and two Sisters for listening to my ranting about this book.

To my Friends who always keep me accompanied.

To the authors who inspire me:

Alice Hoffman
Christopher Paolini
Cressida Cowell
Frances Hodgson Burnett
Fritz Kredel
Grace Lin
Jane Austen
J.K. Rowling
Kate DiCamillo
Lois Lowry
Madeleine L'Engle
Marissa Meyers
Neil Gaiman
Ransom Riggs
Tui T. Sutherland
Veronica Roth

About the Author

Elliana Leigh was born and spent most of her childhood in Indonesia. At age 9, she moved to Washington State and began writing. This collection of stories is Leigh's debut book and was written between the ages of 11 and 14. Elliana Leigh is writing a novel, growing her business, **Crummy Illustrations**, and starting high school in the fall of 2024. She loves reading, dirt biking, and annoying her younger siblings.

Foreword

Elliana Leigh is a remarkable young writer—gifted with a non-stop vivid imagination, a leaning toward the fantastical, and boundless energy. She is also a natural story-teller, as this collection proves. Heaven only knows what she may accomplish in the future, but her readers will be eager to find out.

—Liz Rosenberg, author of *Monster Mama*

POLYPETALOUS

Elliana Leigh

Playground Fear

Sophie blew the loose chalk dust off her pavement drawing, then leaned back to see better. The purple giraffe stared dully at some distant point beyond her shoulder. With a grimace she pulled her sleeve over her hand and rubbed the picture away into a bright smear. Sitting back, Sophie beat the purple out of her shirt and reached for a long piece of red chalk. Hearing a commotion nearby, she glanced up with mild interest. She could see three kids arguing over the rights to a soccer ball with a boy wearing jeans and a red t-shirt. Sophie watched from a distance as she tried reading their lips, when suddenly one of the kids from the group punched the boy in the mouth. Wide-eyed, she watched in growing excitement as the dispute turned into a full-fledged fight. With concern, she watched them attacking the victim who had fallen to the asphalt with aggressive kicks. Slowly, she pushed herself off her knees onto her toes, craning her neck, her fingers tentatively pressing the ground in a running pose.

Sophie pursed her lips and leaned forward, prepared to go and help the single boy, when she felt a tingling on her left wrist. Turning her head, she squinted, her eyes barely seeing the wispy figure.

"What do you need, Trepidation?" Sophie remarked in agitation.

Trepidation hovered quietly beside Sophie before shrugging. "If you help him, you're not helping yourself."

"He needs assistance."

"Still, if you help, it won't do anything," said Trepidation, wavering at Sophie's uncertainty.

Under her gaze, Trepidation's face changed like a holographic Pokémon card in the light, one moment lips quivering in anxiety, the next smiling odiously, eyes crinkling in joyful expectation.

Sophie's mind went in nauseous spirals and swirls; sighing, she sat back down in the shadows and continued drawing, ignoring the fight nearby, with Trepidation's arms wrapped around her, keeping her arrogant and afraid.

Memories

Liam's first memory was standing in front of his preschool introducing himself, telling them that his name was Liam Moore and he had two golden dogs named Cinnamon and Smiley. His second memory was when he was 5 and making crafts with his grandma, a snowman made with pompoms and pipe cleaners.

His third memory, also in kindergarten, was in music class, singing "The Star Spangled Banner" for Veterans Day.

Memories came in like the tide around first grade. His teachers, his friends, his pets, his family. His head was like a bowl and a faucet poured the memories into his mind. His new little brother, his first bike, his favorite fast food restaurant, and licking drippy ice cream from a soggy cone during the Fourth of July parade. He remembered how, in third grade, he told his friends he had a girlfriend. He remembered his father's laugh and five o'clock shadow; he remembered his mother's smile and how she seemed to dance when she cleaned the kitchen. He remembered how white his brother's first tooth was and how he learned to crawl when he was 5 months old.

Memories sweet like nerds from a cardboard box —the first time he kissed Kimberly Brown in fourth grade, the Easter bunny bringing him a basket of chocolate eggs, and the Christmas where everybody was laughing and his father and mother kissed underneath the mistletoe, the room dressed in red, blue, green, and yellow lights.

Memories bitter like black licorice—the times he got spanked for misbehaving, the first time he picked up his baby brother and how he cried, the time he made his mom cry when he split his head open and needed stitches, and how his best friend Billy told him he was stupid in fifth grade. He remembered middle school, how he made and lost friends, his first real girlfriend, and how everyone was bullied or a bully. He remembered his grandma's funeral and how they put her casket and headstone next to his grandpa's, how he couldn't seem to cry and hid in his room the rest of the day in his black suit, clutching his snow-man against his chest. How his heart ached for her that year until she seemed to disappear for good. He remembered being in eighth grade and feeling like the king of the school, how he bullied those smaller than him, and always felt a pinch of guilt afterwards but continued. He remembered first walking into the high school awed by the size of the building.

The memories became happy again. How he was a star student, how he finally told Billy that he didn't want to be friends, how he kissed Ashley Miller in the library, and how excited he was when his parents told him about the new little girl they adopted. The mem-ories soft and sweet as a warm peach—how he and 4 year old Abigail played patty cake, how he and his brother Elijah played basketball on the asphalt in front of the house, how he asked his dad how his day was and the smile he received, and how his mother hugged him when he handed her a Mother's Day gift. High school passed in a blur. He remembered walking on a stage in black robes and a mortarboard, how he shook the principal's hand and took his diploma, and how he gave his speech of thanks to the community that formed him. He remembered going to nursing school. He remembered meeting Ashley Miller again and he fell in love more than ever. He remembered kissing her in their apartment.

The memories now were soft like a summer rain —how he proposed to her after his shift in the hospital, his blue scrubs pressing onto the cold wet concrete as he knelt before Ashley holding out a topaz ring, how he lifted her veil and kissed her in her sparkly white dress at their wedding, how he stroked her face during their honeymoon in Bali. He remembered their first house and him holding a key and her warm hand. He remembered coming home from work and crying in the living room, how she walked in from the kitchen and held him in her arms while he choked out how a young boy he had been taking care of had passed away. He remembered how his mother and father kissed him when he came to visit them in their new country house. Memories flooded his head, the terrifying call he got from Abigail and how he flew to Texas on the first flight he could find, how he held his dying brother's hand until the heart monitor stopped beeping, how the funeral for Elijah seemed like the end of the world, how Abigail cried into her boyfriend's arms and my parents stood as still as statues clutching each other's hands.

How I wept saying it was my fault and how Ashley looked me in the eyes and told me it was the drunk driver's fault, not mine. I remembered going home after a few weeks and how I slowly healed. I remembered Ashley kissing my cheek and telling me she was pregnant. I remembered pressing my cheek to her stomach and feeling the baby kick. I remembered sitting next to Ashley's hospital bed and looking at the face of our new daughter. The years and memories seemed to fly by, how we had two more children after Rose, and how we named them John and Lucas. How tiring it was to change their diapers, feed them and keep them safe, but how rewarding it was to hear their laughter and earn their trust, to hear them call me Daddy and call Ashley Mommy. I remembered my father and mother being called Grandpa and

Grandma and how my parents loved their grandchildren. I remembered how happy my sister Abigail was on her wedding day, saying the vows of marriage to her love. Sad and happy memories started to mix, Abigail's first child, my parents' funerals, me and Ashley's sixteenth anniversary, Abigail's divorce, and watching my children grow up. I remembered tearing up when I saw Rose in black robes at her high school graduation and her loving smile. I remembered watching my two sons leave the house like Rose. I remembered my children's weddings and first houses. I remembered Abigail and her son traveling around Europe for his 17th birthday. I remembered retiring and staying home with my loyal and loving wife.

The memories grow into a lifetime. Rose and her husband's first child, me being called Grandpa and Ashley being Grandma. I remember family Christmas and bouncing my grandchildren on my old knees. I remember growing very old and weak. I remember taking medication and kissing Ashley's wrinkled forehead and her saying she didn't want to lose me. I remember watching TV on the couch with my family. I remember the Christmas where I kissed Ashley underneath the mistletoe. I remember celebrating our

58th anniversary. I remember getting too old and coughing until I couldn't breathe. I remember laying on my death bed surrounded by my family, waiting for the remembering to end.

"Daniel?!" came an excited voice nearby.

I let out a groan, peel open my eyes, and stare in shock at the woman with bright red hair.

"Daniel!!" cries the woman in happiness, kissing my face over and over again.

"Where's Ashley? Where's my wife?" I ask, struggling to sit up.

The woman looks confused but still happy, "I'm your wife, and I don't believe you know any Ashleys."

I look at the red-haired woman in panic. "You're not my wife! You're not Ashley. You're not my sister or daughter!"

"Daniel, calm down, let me call the doctor."

"My name is not Daniel!"

"Yes it is," she says, pressing a button nearby then leaning back towards me. "You're 33 year old Daniel Brown, and I'm your wife Mia, we have a 9 year old son and two cats. Do you remember now?"

I start to cry in confusion. "No. I am 83 year old Liam Moore, my wife's name is Ashley, I have three children named Rose, John, and Lucas, and seven grandchildren and no pets."

The red-haired woman starts silently sobbing just as a doctor and four other people walk in the room.

"Mia, baby, what's wrong?" cries one of the people, an old lady.

"He doesn't remember us!" cries the woman called Mia.

"I didn't say that," I remark, drawing their attention to me. "I just said you are not my wife, because you're just a dream. I dreamt this before."

"Dan, this isn't a dream," says the doctor softly. "You've been in a coma. Reality can get confused when you're unconscious as long as you were."

I open my mouth to tell him he's wrong but I feel a surge of recognition when I look closely at the crying redhead. My wife. I remember suddenly. I recognize the old woman calming Mia as her mom. My own mother and father stand next to my 9 year old son, Jacob. I remember I never had siblings and that I am a young man still in his prime. I remember that this is my family, and realize Ashley and the rest of my Liam Moore life was never real. "Mia." I say softly, reaching for her hand.

Her sobs turn to sniffles, and she sees the recognition in my eyes. Letting out a cry of joy she wraps her arms around my neck and kisses me; I kiss her back.

I kiss Mia, my wife, but I miss my true love, Ashley, dearly.

Crow

There once was a king and a queen in an ancient, beautiful kingdom. They had a son but no daughter. Then, to everyone's unexpected joy, the queen was found to be with child. However, when the child was born, it was on Day of the Unlucky and their happiness faded. Usually, if a child was born on this day of the year, the parents would leave the baby in the forest, as to keep their village from being plagued by bad luck. But since the young girl was born of royalty, she was allowed to live to adulthood.

However good the intentions were, keeping the princess alive was cruel to the princess and the villagers. The citizens had sacrificed their own children born on the Day of the Unlucky for the good of the village and were angered and crushed that the king and queen would not do the same.

The girl, meanwhile, was unlucky and ill-treated by the servants. Her food was always served spoiled, and her water dirty. She was constantly hurting herself; her parents were too busy to love her or notice how the servants treated her and how everyone shunned her. So she lived in a constant state of misery throughout her childhood.

Then, one fateful day, a neighboring kingdom attacked her home. The Unlucky Princess's kingdom was quickly defeated and only the young princess made it out alive. The girl was sad but not devastated because her old home held no good memories. She wandered around for months until she found a nest of fledglings with a crow keeping them warm. The young princess wept, wishing she had a mother who loved her. The moment the wish entered her mind she transformed into a young crow. She squawked in terror, unsure what had happened. The mother crow in the tree heard the princess's cries. She flew down to get the little crow and brought her up to her warm nest. The princess was shocked as the three crow fledglings greeted her with cries of joy. The young girl had found a home with those who loved her.

Slowly, the months went by. She learned to fly and learned to expect the unexpected. One day, while flying through the air with her bird family, she spotted a bush covered with plump berries. Squawking with pleasure at her find, she flew down and ate her share, saving the rest for her mother and siblings. Hopping along the ground, she saw her reflection in a dewdrop on a blade of grass. It was not her bird self but her human self. When she tilted her head the girl in the reflection also tilted her head. With a sudden burst of pity for the miserable girl trapped in the dewdrop she pecked the dewdrop off the grass and let it splash across the soil. She then took off to join her new family in the sky.

Consequences of War

Svetlana glanced nervously at the papers clutched in her frost-bitten fingers. She and her two brothers were headed to Siberia so they could be safe from the German soldiers invading Russia. Svetlana glanced at Nikolai and Boris who were fighting clumsily with dead sticks. "сейчас не время играть!![1]" she cried, tucking her identification papers in her coat pocket.

Jumping down from the rickety wagon she strode toward her brothers, holding their thick jackets. "тебе

---

[1] *"Now is not the time to play!"*

нужно согреться,[2]" Svetlana said harshly, smacking the mossy sticks away and forcing a coat on Boris, who cried in dismay and pulled the jacket on himself. Nikolai grumbled, snatched his coat from his sister, and put it on. Then grabbing their small hands, Svetlana marched them back towards the slowly moving wagon.

December 1, 1941

Nikolai and Boris do not seem to comprehend the danger we are in from Germany. Mama would have known what to do. I miss Tatyana, Sasha, and my other friends dearly, especially when we were twirling like snowflakes on the ice with our beautiful skates.

December 3, 1941

Nikolai and Boris were very naughty and went on a thinly iced pond. A man in our small group barely managed to get them off before the ice cracked. I refused to let them off the wagon the rest of the day. I swear I felt like paddling them like Papa did when they were bad.

December 7, 1941

While traveling on the icy road, I saw bodies of children, women, men, and wagon animals mangled near the trees next to

---

[2] *"You need to warm up,"*

the road. They looked as if they had been blown to bits by a
bomb. Luckily, Nikolai and Boris were engaged in an argument
and did not see this horror the war had so savagely created. The
fear that makes me shudder is wondering if this will happen to us.

December 8, 1941
Their soldiers are bold
Their hearts are cold
I will not be sold
to evil falsehoods of the Wehrmacht

December 11, 1941
Nikolai and Boris are becoming young men, or so they say. Today
they carried five pieces of wood each to the fire. Nikolai is turning
8 soon, and it is my responsibility as the eldest to give him a gift to
remind him to grow responsible for his own actions.

December 15, 1941
Nikolai is now 8. It gives me both joy and grief. He has sur-
vived another year, yet he has had to live in this evil war since he
was 6. When will it end? As for his gift: words of wisdom.

December 18, 1941
Today, me and the rest of the girls cut off our long braids to

make ropes to fix the wagon.

December 20, 1941

I wonder often if I shall die young or old, painfully or quietly. You may say these are morbid thoughts, but I can tell you, every-one is thinking the same thing.

December 22, 1941

It has been six months since Germany invaded Russia, forcing us to flee to the countryside of Siberia. Six months since Mama and Papa died. Six months and twenty-six days since I turned 11. Life will have to persevere or die.

December 25, 1941

There used to be a holiday in Russia called Christmas, but it was banned thirteen years before I was born. I heard that during that holiday you would decorate a pine tree with candles and tinsel, then give out gifts of toys, clothes, and trinkets, then lastly have a big and special dinner. Christmas sounds like a holiday that our country needs. Especially now.

December 30, 1941

Nikolai and Boris are brats! Sometimes I am convinced they are little Leshies disguised as adorable little boys. They ate all of the potatoes that I cooked! So now I have nothing to eat today.

December 31, 1941
Tomorrow is New Year's.

January 1, 1942
My New Year's resolution is to accept everyone with an open heart, we all should.

January 4, 1942
Boris had a nightmare last night of Papa's last moments. I'm saddened that he remembers this for he was 3 then, and had turned 4 while on our trek to Siberia. Curiously and with great trepidation, I asked if he remembers Mama's death. He replied that he did not. I silently let out a prayer of thanks to some un-known god. For Papa was only shot, but Mama's death was worse than many people's worst nightmares. That is what this war has done.

January 7, 1942
Two members of our party froze to death last night. Me, Nikolai, and Boris are lucky enough to have thick garments and each other for warmth.

January 11, 1942

Our group is losing faith in our survival.

January 13, 1942

The closer we get to our destination the fewer horrors I see. No more bodies half buried in snow or bloody trails along the roads, and that is pure relief. I've shielded as much as I could from Nikolai and Boris but sometimes there were bodies in piles for miles. That scars the mind.

January 17, 1942

I was walking in the woods today, scavenging for something in the wintry forest to eat, when I came across a sock. It was small enough to fit a tiny babe's foot. I let out gasping sobs as I looked at the tiny sock. Bending down, I saw a tiny leg. Slowly, I brushed aside the snow and looked at the frozen corpse: the tiny fingernails, the blue lips, and duckling down hair. Silently, I covered the abandoned baby once more with snow and said a few comforting words to ease their tender spirit.

January 21, 1942

Are we all condemned to death by this ridiculous war? Are we forsaken because of some anger within someone high in power? All I wish is that this war shall end as well as Adolf Hitler.

Dreams aren't always sweet, nor am I. I lost my innocence in June of 1941. Now I only hold the determination to survive and the loyalty to my brothers.

January 23, 1942

I thought life was a blessing
Now I'm second guessing
overwhelmed with grief
Adolf Hitler the thief
Of my joy
A truly evil ploy

January 25, 1942

We are half starved, and a woman in her mid-twenties keeps looking at Boris with a ravenous, crazy look in her eye. She licked her lips whenever she spied his dark hair among the group. I'm staying on watch tonight with a knife I've hidden in my pocket.

January 26, 1942

We were walking later in the afternoon today when the young woman who had been eyeing Boris leapt towards him with a scythe in hand and a bloodcurdling, hungry scream. Quickly, I pulled the blade from my pocket and drove it into her chest as she descended towards Boris. I twisted the knife bitterly and drew back, shielding my brothers behind me. Baba Yaga bled to death slowly with everyone watching. Then the woman grew limp, the second person I have killed since June.

January 28, 1942

Boris is avoiding me and is instead staying with two siblings I have scarcely talked to. Me killing someone scared Boris. Nikolai was a little shaken but otherwise unfazed; he's seen me kill someone before. The event makes me ponder if there are any more Baba Yagas among us.

January 31, 1942

It is almost February. We are almost there. We are almost safe.

February 1, 1942

There has been a shift in the atmosphere. Before I was coddled and asked constantly of my state. After the woman's murder, I received only glares of fear and lack of needed comfort.

February 3, 1942

Where do we go when we die?

Svetlana looked up from her loose sheaf of papers. Nikolai looked at her grimly.

"What брат[3]?" she asked.

"They're planning something, Ana. The others." He inclined his head toward the rest of their group.

"COWARDS! вы, кровожадные свиньи[4]!" Svetlana screamed, tears streaming down her face, straining herself angrily towards the small party. The rope tied securely around her wrists and to a handle on the steamer trunk did not break or fray. "пожалуйста[5]," she begged, falling to her knees, shaking her dark head.

"Svetlana, caretaker of Nikolai and Boris, we condemn you to death for the murder of Katerina. Consider this your punishment," droned a blond man twenty feet from her.

"No!" screamed Nikolai thrashing in the group's many arms, struggling to get to her. The blond man forced Nikolai into the wagon next to Boris where he continued to hold him.

---

[3] *brother*

[4] *bloodthirsty pigs*

[5] *Please*

"Ana!" her loyal brother wailed before throwing curses and obscenities at his restrainer. Boris just watched.

The group and wagon slowly moved away, Nikolai yelling her name over and over again. Sobbing, Svetlana looked at Boris, his bright blue eyes met hers, he hid his face in terror.

"I WAS PROTECTING YOU!" she screamed, the veins in her neck bulging, "Я обещал[6]!" The blood vessels in her eyes popped and her dark, shaggy hair fell across her dirty face, giving her a crazed look. The wagon and people went around a bend and out of sight.

Whimpering, Svetlana curled up onto the steamer trunk, the wind biting through her thin cotton dress and pants. They had taken her warm garments for the others in the party, leaving her to freeze to death in simple worn clothes.

Svetlana
It's been a day, at least I think.

---

[6] *"I promised!"*

Svetlana

I'm cold and can't stop shivering or yawning. And I keep hearing Mama. I found a sapling. I put it in the trunk with some dirt to keep it warm.

Svetlana

It's hot, I feel like I am sweating, but I'm not. Isn't that strange? And I don't shiver anymore. It must almost be summer, but there's snow piled in great drifts, it's strange.

Svetlana

I'm so hungry my stomach is eating itself.

Svetlana

Hi, my name is Svetlana, I had a mama, papa, and two brothers. I've killed two people to protect my two brothers. The tips of my fingers are black. Where do we go when we die?

Svetlana lay on the steamer trunk with a yawn, and she never woke again. Slowly, the sapling she planted in the chest grew up, breaking through wood, fabric, and bones, wrapping its roots around the young girl as if cradling her soul.

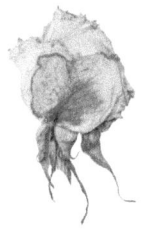

The Tunnel

Our city was built on the tunnel. Our ancestors thought that perhaps something special was in the tunnel that would bless the city they were to build. However, anyone who entered the tunnel never came out, and anyone who peered in the tunnel became insane, often speaking of evil, malevolent beasts, and how the cursed screamed in terror in the tunnel. We lost hundreds in a space of weeks, either to the tunnel or from the cursed killing themselves. So our city was named 'Onakele City' meaning 'Corrupt City.' We who lived in the city called ourselves the Abesabayo, *the afraid;* but, however scared we were of our new home, we didn't leave, for outside the city a Great War had ravaged the lands and left molten metal that refused to cool, nuclear changed animals, rivers of lava, sinkholes thousands of feet deep and wide, dangerous fumes and 'Ababi' or 'the evil ones.' The Ababi were said to be humans so utterly changed they looked like the monsters from your worst nightmares. No one has seen an Ababi up close, only from a distance, for even if you found yourself fifty feet from one, you faced an inevitable death. The pungent fear of our people seemed to make clouds of their own, beside the looming red clouds that forever hung in the sky. Clouds of blood. 'Impi Yokugcina' or 'The Last War' was said to be the greatest world war ever. For us, it rarely rains water, whereas blood is rained upon us daily. Blood of the same people who died during the fifty years of Impi Yokugcina rains on us decades later.

My name is Aliyah. That's all. A common street urchin among the dirty and dangerous Onakele city. I am more fortunate than most. Or not. Is it fortunate to be alive or not? I do not know because I have not lived another life to compare to my current life. This is what

I know: the waft of death, of wolves tearing apart my stomach from the inside, of isolation, of feeling out of control, of the sticky blood that lines my throat, of being constantly tired and sick, and complete freedom. The freedom of being able to steal and kill without being hanged or jailed by the law, for there is no government system, everyone is for themselves. I know who my parents are, I'm a mirror image of my mother. She is young, not yet in her thirties. My father is a guess I made. He is a balding, fat man in his late sixties who smokes two packs of cigarettes a day; he constantly beats my mother with his fists. I feel no sympathy, for no one is family by blood but by dedication. I myself was raised as a babe by an 8 year old girl named Dilemma, or Emma for short. She called me Aliyah, for Aliyah has the first three letters of alive. Emma was beaten to death when I was 6. Been on my own since.

Here in Onakele City, you avoid being noticed at all costs. If you are beautiful or notable, you will be dead before the sun wakes. Most travel around the city at night, more likely to survive that way. Pale blonde hair like mine is dangerous, dye it black then you turn from a star in the dark to another shadow. Becoming vain about your looks is as stupid as cutting your own throat to prove to someone you're not a coward. Blend in and you live. Simple. Also, you constantly hold weapons; if you don't have one, you're clearly an idiot. This world isn't for the perfect, it was made for pure savages. Like me. Like everyone in this cursed world. Tip: carry at least three knives and a bat. We're not total savages, however. Pure—yes. Total—no. We trade for the more important stuff like food, clothes, or protection. I read in a history book once that people back then would fight over pieces of ore shaped into little discs that were bright yellow, and floppy green pieces of paper. Apparently, people back then were utter fools. Who would want coins or dollars when you could have food? Morons.

No one does funerals here. Want to die? Walk in the tunnel. Die before then? Your body rots and is eaten by the rabid dogs, feral cats, starving pigs, and vultures. Only the strongest survive.

There is one rule in this hell: never utter the word ~~inunu~~. Someone did once and nearly destroyed us all. ~~Inunu~~. The tunnel. Impi Yokugcina. They're all connected, they nearly destroyed the world; that is our legacy.

Grim Reaper

Many, many, many years ago there was an orphaned boy named Reaper. He was tall and gangly. While the other residents of the village had dark complexions, Reaper had come from somewhere else and had white skin. Befuddled, the village took this child into the orphan home, with no knowledge of where he came from.

Reaper worked in the village's plentiful fields with a scythe in hand. If you asked him where he came from he would answer, "I don't know." Most assumed he was lying, but indeed he had lost his memory with no hope of recovering it.

After working in the fields for two years he requested to be a gravedigger. Reaper asked for this role because of the familiar feeling of death that surrounded the area. It made him depressed to walk over the bodies of once living people, but he had an unexplainable urge to tend to the wafting souls of the cemetery.

Wearing a black cloak with a pointed top and a scythe and shovel in hand he marched solemnly to the graveyard. Working day after day, night after night. People were spooked with the uncanny motivation of Reaper. With terror and bitterness, the village people called him Grim Reaper, for never once had they seen a smile on his face.

Finally, after five years, the distrust gave way to a roaring anger. They suspected Grim Reaper was attacking their loved ones' souls and tying their own souls to the devil's wickedness.

Tragically misunderstood, they drove Grim Reaper out of their village, bleeding and bruised. During the commotion, the mob accidentally set fire to their town. Only a few escaped the burning rubble and smoke, each spreading vicious rumors and lies about the Grim Reaper to the surrounding villages.

Rejected from society, Grim Reaper worked in secret. Even now, most people believe he is a heartless monster, and few believe the truth: that he was an ordinary person doing the work of burying and honoring the dead.

The Forgotten Knight

An injured warrior lay on crumbling brown grass in a forgotten war field littered with bodies without souls. For two days, he remained unmoved. His mouth was dry like the brittle winter air. His body armor reduced to metal scraps with cold fingers of frost inching across the gray melted ore. The battle had been sorely lost, and he had been left like a useless dog abandoned by its owner. And so it was that he awoke on the night after the second day, cloaked by the dark horizon, moonbeams, and starlight. Baffled and fearful.

Bartholomew was a farm boy, nothing special beyond growing crops and keeping livestock. Bartholomew was the son of Benedict the son of Baldwin and so on; a long line of farmers. Bartholomew was often called Theo by his family and surrounding cousins. He was a strong boy from a young age and cunning. And so it was that when the need for knights arose, Bartholomew volunteered eagerly. It was a way to forever honor his family's line. Theo quickly rose through the ranks and became an honored warrior. He had been in plenteous skirmishes, ambushes, and small battles, but never a war, and when he finally fought in one he was wounded and left for the enemy.

When Bartholomew awoke on the second day he moved swiftly, knowing the other kingdom would surely be bringing the wagons for their dead. They would discover him alive and kill him without mercy.

He dragged himself to his feet and limped quickly towards the safety of the towering forest. Theo relaxed his tense muscles once he was in the wood's leafy arms. Then he stripped himself of his reflective armor, grabbed a walking stick, and trudged in the general direction of his kingdom.

Theo had been walking through the woods for weeks.

He would have died if he could not hunt or identify edible wild plants. He would have been lonely if he had not found a wandering, mangy kitten. It had a rusty orange coat with stripes on its face, legs, and tail, and circular markings on its back and stomach.

Bartholomew avoided towns and traded venison and hides to traveling merchants, acquiring a white tunic, black pants, boots, a gray leather vest, a belt, and lastly, a hat to keep the sun off his head. With his wounds healing, comfortable clothes, food, and some company from his pet, he ventured onward to home.

Smiling happily, he trotted quickly towards the stronghold gates to the castle of the Pouvior Kingdom. Beside Bartholomew was Ophelia who had grown from a chubby, pencil-tailed kitten to a beautiful, sleek cat. Upon Theo's back was a light pack, holding some food and water but nothing more. He approached the gates with joy. Four guards were posted along with those poised on top of the castle walls.

"Hello, it's me, Bartholomew," he said, slowing down and eyeing the soldier's suddenly raised swords.

"Is that so, spy?" spat one of the armored men.

Theo blinked, startled. "I'm not a spy."

"That's what the others said," answered the man,

ending the conversation as he charged towards him. The other men followed in pursuit while the men on the wall showered arrows in his direction.

Bartholomew ran away like a coward and cursed his own stupidity, for who would believe a dead man?

Bartholomew wandered aimlessly in the forest near the plains where he had fought. He had nowhere to go. Towns didn't trust strangers during wars. His family's farm was invaded and they were all killed. The castle believed that General Bartholomew was dead. Sadly, he sang a lullaby his sister had sung to him when they explored together hand in hand.

"Tiptoe past the fields known,
traipse past home and hither to the place undisclosed,
secrets lurk not shown,
disown the rules and onward to the unknown."

A tear ran down his sloped nose and dripped off the end. Silently weeping, Theo picked up Ophelia and cradled her against his chest, humming sea shanties and old nursery rhythms.

He wandered through the woods looking at towering alders with autumn leaves like maple syrup and caramel. Ophelia patiently walked beside Theo as he stared awestruck at the beautiful trees. He had traveled far from the places he had known, having gone off to explore like he wanted to do all his life.

Bartholomew was stunned at the views, the towering mountains he had climbed, the enormous rivers he had crossed, and the freedom he had felt. He heard a singing that flowed with a burbling stream nearby. Walking softly, he and Ophelia peeked around a large alder. There was a young woman with light brown skin and glossy black hair with wooden beads strung through it, and she was dressed in a simple dress dyed a light blue. She was bent over a stream collecting water.

"Hello," Theo remarked, stepping forward.

Hurriedly the girl leaped back and doused him with water from her jar.

He gasped at the sudden cold while the girl tilted her head curiously. "Hi-i-i, I'm The-e-eo." His teeth were chattering and gave her a slight bow.

A smile started on the girl's perfect lips, and her eyes sparkled curiously. Then, lifting her eyebrows, she leaned forward and gave him a quick kiss on the cheek.

Bartholomew stared in shock as the young woman's shoulders shook with quiet laughter as she took in his startled expression. Ophelia mewed loudly to claim her rightful attention. The girl jumped back in shock, then laughed again and leaned down to inspect the fierce little creature.

"Are you okay, my Theo?" asked Aiyana, brushing Bartholomew's golden curls from his face.

"Of course, my flower," he replied, kissing her on her soft brown forehead.

She blushed, toyed with her blue dress, and leaned against him.

The other Tallulah tribe members had a hard time adapting to him, but Aiyana was the chief's daughter and she was allowed to keep her Theo.

The Dance of the Flowers

nce upon a time, there was a girl named Moonflower who loved the boy in the woods. Everyone called Moonflower reckless and stupid for trusting and loving a stranger, but she paid them no heed and visited her love every night the moon was in the sky.

Moonflower called him Sunflower for he had golden hair that matched the color of the sun. Sunflower could not talk and could not write so he could not tell Moonflower his real name. Moonflower never talked when she was with Sunflower, instead she shared with him in his silence.

One night when the moon was high in the night sky they laid upon a soft green hill pointing out the constellations in the sky, when nearby they heard a voice speak.

"Pretty young girl, what are you doing with my slave?"

Moonflower jumped in shock while fear shone in Sunflower's eyes.

A gorgeous woman stared at them angrily. "I give you shelter and food and this is how you repay me?" she spat at Sunflower.

Moonflower saw the pendant of a star upon the woman's chest and knew she was a witch. Grabbing Sunflower's hand she ran as fast as she could, her white dress snapping in the wind. But the witch was close, chasing her slave and his love.

Sunflower stopped Moonflower in a field sur-rounded by forest and spoke his first words, the words of a spell that turned them into flowers.

The witch tasted magic in the air, then stopping before them she cast a spell on the lovers. The witch pulled out an hourglass and placed it on the ground. "Every year, one grain of sand will fall. Until the bottom is completely full and there isn't a grain left on the top… you will be under my curse." The lady witch smiled with pink lips, her brown hair blowing in the wind, then she got up and left the lovers entrapped in their spell, for Moonflower could only become human at night while Sunflower could only become human during the day. Until every last grain of sand in the hourglass went to the bottom, Moonflower and Sunflower would never again be human together.

1966

Becca Evans unwound the licorice of her Catherine Wheel, eating the pungent sweet treat with delight. She skipped as she ate the candy, her school bag thumping against her hip and the large clasps on the bag clanking. Becca finished her treat just as she reached the school gate.

Slowing down, she looked around for her best friend, Robert Williams. Spotting him, she ran over. "Hi, Robert!" she exclaimed, linking her arm with his.

"Hi, Becca," said Robert, pulling his trousers higher up.

"Mom made me put on stockings today, and

they're so itchy!" she complained, scratching her legs.

Robert just kept sucking the gum-ball in his mouth.

Annoyed, Becca tried again. "How do you like my dress?" she said, swishing her navy blue dress with a white collar and red bow tie.

Robert looked at her then shrugged. "I don't like how many buttons it has, but I like the matching red headband," he replied, going back to his sucking.

Frowning, Becca tapped one of her white buttons before disregarding the whole thing. Skipping, her arm still linked to Robert's, she sang a nursery rhyme:

> *"Gee up little horse, carrying us two,*
> *Over the mountain to gather nuts,*
> *Water in the river, the stones are slippery,*
> *We both fall down, well what a trick!"*

Becca beamed happily as her shiny black shoes made a tap, tap, tap sound on the tile. Together, the two best friends made their way to Mrs. Lewis's class.

"Morning, Miss Evans. Morning, Master William, sit down and take out your textbooks please," said Mrs. Lewis, tilting her head.

"Mrs. Lewis looks like her suit is spun out of pink

candy floss!" giggled Becca behind her hand. Robert nodded in agreement. Sitting down she pulled out her subtraction and addition book, then pulled out her lucky pink pencil, humming all the while.

Students filled in the room quickly, scrambling to get to their seats. Mrs. Lewis took her place before the chalkboard just as the bell rang long and loud. Mrs. Lewis paced before the classroom taking roll call before telling them about their upcoming holiday. "You will be dismissed at noon today," droned Mrs. Lewis. "Until then, let class begin."

Just as they were about to start, Robert raised his hand.

"Yes, Master William," sighed Mrs. Lewis.

"I have to go to the bathroom!" Robert pleaded, wiggling in his seat.

"Go quickly," grumbled Mrs. Lewis.

Robert leaped out of his seat to the bathroom, like a kangaroo using a jump rope.

Becca slouched in her seat, she hated starting class late—it took away from their recess time and always meant she was the last one to the swing set.

Then she felt a rumble under her feet and heard shrieking and shouting outside the school. Curious, she glanced out the window that faced the courtyard. Nothing there—just hula hoops, jump ropes, and hopscotch lines drawn with chalk. Then she turned to the window facing the mountain just as Mrs. Lewis began to scream. Outside, coming down the mountain towards their town, was a landslide of black rocks. Coal.

"GET UNDER YOUR DESKS AND COVER YOUR HEADS!" yelled Mrs. Lewis, frantically shoving kids off their chairs and under their tables.

Becca slid under her desk and covered her head with her arms. "MOM! DAD!" she screamed in terror, tears rolling down her face as she trembled like a wind caught leaf.

"ROBERT!" Becca yelled, desperately crawling from under her table and rushing towards the classroom door.

"BECCA!" screamed Mrs. Lewis, reaching for her.

Becca heard the coal hissing towards the school, heard it break the glass into tinkling shards, as it smashed and tumbled into the desks, and she felt it slam into her side and bury her instantly. The coal seemed to crush every ounce of air out of her lungs as she frantically tried to breathe in, but there was nothing to breathe except coal dust. Gasping like a fish, she tried to move the heavy coal off her crushed ribs but her arms were immobile. Slowly, she felt herself suffocate.

"Help," she whispered with her remaining strength, then the world faded into ebony darkness.

At 9:13 in the morning on October 21, 1966, a landslide of coal crushed a small Welsh mining town killing 144 people. 28 adults and 116 children.

Pepper Dragon

The little pepper dragon hatched knowing his name was Habanero. Unfurling his bright yellow wings the tiny dragon let out a whistle, then used his four miniature claws to scurry into the foliage of his hatching tree. The scales on his snout were dark red then faded into light orange towards the tip of his tail. The end of his tail was fuzzy yellow and soft like down. The wings were built for gliding not flying and were thin and velvety. His pupils were pitch black, the irises a bright green like a tomato stalk, and the scleras were a very light green. His teeth, talons, and horns were jade white, and the small round spikes that ran along his head, neck, back, and tail were also white. He looked like a dangerous version of a small cute lizard.

The hatching tree was three small trees intertwined into a braid that made the trunk; the bushy top was made of small snaking branches covered in triangular leaves of blue-silver. The wood of the tree was gnarled and a rich honey color. The tree was only six feet tall and had thin curved peppers hanging from the end of the branches in bunches. The peppers were actually pepper dragon eggs. Dragons aren't like mammals, reptiles, or any other class. Dragons grow *from* the tree, grown to protect the tree, and the tree in return gives the tiny dragons shelter. Pepper dragons are hatched the size of a common house gecko and grow to the size of a tabby cat. They are as dangerous and intelligent as humans.

The peppers were red, orange, yellow, white, green, and purple, all varying in different shades.

Another pepper dragon hatched knowing her name was Cayenne. She looked like her brother but her body was a dark purple and her wings and fuzzy tail tip a pale lilac. Her irises were golden and her scleras a light yellow. Her forked pink tongue flicked out, tasting the air before she joined her brother in the leaves.

More pepper dragons hatched knowing their names. The entirely white dragon was Ghost, the two headed green dragon was Jalapeño and Poblano, the yellow dragon was Anaheim, the orange dragon was Tabasco, and the red dragon was Carolina. They were from the same pepper bunch as Habanero and Cayenne, and were sibling-bonded.

The six of them scurried up to the first two that hatched. The other pepper bunches had hatched. There had been five pepper bunches in total.

One of the pepper dragon groups chose to dig dens underground beneath the tree's roots, another group wove little hanging homes out of grass that hung from the branches of the tree and looked like weaver bird nests. The third group made little clay ledges on the trunk that they padded with moss, the fourth group made their home in the hollow of the trunk where the three winding trees left an empty space, and the last group made little nests in the foliage of the tree. All the dragons plucked the small berries that looked like star fruit from the tree's branches and ate them, then they went into their nests and went to sleep.

The next morning all the pepper dragons met at the base of the tree, poking their noses curiously into a nearby stream, and watching fish leap around like acrobats.

The pepper dragon tree was in a meadow surrounded by giant redwood trees, creeks crisscrossed around the grassy plain like small rivers. The meadow was dotted with many flowers such as zinnias, bluebells, dahlias, foxglove, fluffy teddy-bear sunflowers, and poppies. And surrounding the pepper dragon tree in great quantities were forget-me-nots and lantana flower bushes. Beside the flowers was cogon grass, ostrich fern, fig trees, and succulents on decaying stumps. It was an isolated paradise.

Quietly, the dragons sat in a circle in front of the hatching tree; sibling sat next to sibling. A soft whistling emanated through the air as the pepper dragons communicated. Terms were set on what sibling groups gathered, hunted, and farmed while the remaining sibling groups attended to and protected the hatching tree.

Habanero, Cayenne, Ghost, Jalapeño-Poblano, Anaheim, Tabasco, and Carolina had the job of gathering. Scurrying up onto the top of the pepper dragon tree they spread their wings and leaped. Pepper dragon dragons don't have wings like bats, they have a patagium, a furry membrane that connects from the wrist to the ankle on both sides. Just like a flying squirrel. Gliding over the ground they headed toward the fig trees. They landed near the base of the fruit tree and wove small bags out of cogon grass before climbing to the purple fruit hanging ripely from the fig tree. You must remember that pepper dragons hatch the size of a gecko. And they hatched just yesterday. The sibling group, instead of harvesting the sweet fruit, burrowed inside the fig and took its seeds, nibbled on a fig before alighting to the top of the tree and gliding back home. Once they reached the hatching tree, they buried the seeds in the cool ground to keep the food fresh.

When the pepper dragons grew too big to live on the tree, they built small underground dens nearby, not under the tree for they were too big. The five sibling groups lived with the tree until they were fully grown, seven years after they had hatched. Then one sibling group after another left until only Habanero remained with his siblings, waiting for the tree to sprout more pepper dragon eggs and hatch the new generation before leaving to have their own fulfilling travels.

Years later, Habanero and his siblings found their way home after many adventures. However, the home they found was not the one they remembered. The giant redwoods laid flat on the ground, stripped of their branches and pine needle crowns. The abundance of flowers and grass swayed in the wind, engulfed in smokey flames, and the fig trees were ablaze, flakes of red ash floating and twirling in the air like vicious fireflies. Through the thick haze, Habanero saw the hatching tree with its blue-silver leaves on fire. The pepper dragons glided down to the tree. Habanero and Cayenne put out the flames with their talons while the others scooped water from the ash-clogged creek onto the hatching tree. When the flames on the tree were put out they searched for further damage. The bark of the tree had been scraped and the roots of the tree exposed and damaged and the bunches of peppers on the end of the branches were burnt to husks. Carefully, the dragons dug up the tree and moved it into a sinkhole that led to the tunnels of a cave—a secluded place they had found in their youth. They planted the tree and nursed it back to health. Then leaving Ghost, Carolina, Anaheim, and Tabasco behind with the hatching tree, Habanero, Jalapeño-Poblano, and Cayenne left, searching the world for other remaining hatching trees and pepper dragons, but found none.

And to this day it is said that Habanero, his siblings, and the hatching tree remain hidden, waiting for the day the tree grows more peppers. Peppers in the colors red, orange, yellow, white, green and purple, all varying in different shades.

Traitors

Calalily was tearing through a forest with Tommy on her back and Bengal, Siberian, Karen, and Sarah running by her side. Behind, they could hear cars and heavy footsteps, and above, small planes. Her brow was slick with sweat and her bare feet stung, but she was too tired to shape-shift. Gasping for air, she spotted a small cave entrance.

"Cave," Calalily managed to groan, alerting the others of the hiding spot.

The little group slid with ease into the small entrance, then Siberian collected her remaining energy and commanded the plants to hide the entrance before collapsing, unconscious. Bengal gathered his sister in his arms and crept to the others while Calalily stayed at the back as they slipped deeper into the cave and temporary safety.

Calalily set her head against the cold cavern floor, remembering how it all started. It had been an ordinary morning. They woke up in their hidden house, did activities, did chores; in the afternoon it went downhill. Karen had unexpectedly yelled at them, questioning why they were hiding.

"Because we're different," replied 7 year old Tommy.

"So?" Karen said, putting her hands on her hips. "We can do 'dangerous' things that other people can't do. It's not like I'm going to use my powers to kill someone." Then she had packed up her bag. Bengal and Siberian following her with bags of their own. A few months later they came running back, telling Calalily, Sarah, and little Tommy that some people were trying to catch them, that they had followed them here, and that they had to run. And they had been on the run for the past Moon, wondering if they would be caught and killed.

Calalily thrashed angrily in their grip. "Let me go!" she shrieked blindly, trying to bite Karen. She transformed into a wolf and sprung out of her grasp, snapping her shiny white teeth at her. Her former friends stared at her lashing tail.

"Listen, Calalily, if we turn you over there's a chance they'll leave us alone. Besides, you don't matter," Karen said, tossing her hair.

"They want all of us. Turning me over won't help," Calalily snarled in her wolf throat.

Karen scoffed. "You're the only one without family, and the most dangerous."

Tommy peered at her, tears rolling down his cheeks as he hugged Sarah. 'Sorry,' he mouthed.

Bengal and Siberian tightly clutched each other's hands, avoiding her stare. Calalily tried to sprint away but a dart hit her in the shoulder, knocking her down.

Calalily spun her strawberry-blonde curls between her hands, boredom filling her head like a murky fog. Her prison consisted of walls, a ceiling, and floor that look identical. "Scared of a 15 year old?" she mocked the hidden speaker and camera.

"Stop it, you're making them angry," hissed Siberian.

The other five were caught as well when they came outside the cave to offer her.

"Who's fault is it that we're here?" Calalily demanded, her voice as cold as the Arctic before leaping up and clawing the spy devices to pieces.

"We have a proposition," Sarah said with a waver in her voice. "If you help us escape, we'll leave you alone."

Calalily thought it through then nodded. "Promise?"

"Promise."

She patiently waited for an escape, ignoring her fellow inmates and giving venomous smiles and scars to those who ventured into the small room. After countless weeks of waiting she and the others escaped. Calalily made sure to traumatize her captors. Then they departed, Bengal and Siberian, Karen, Sarah and Tommy, and Calalily on her own.

Car Crash

She opened her eyes, her lids feeling like they were lifting heavy stones. She could hear nothing except a buzzing, like a hive of angry bees around her head. Everything she saw was unclear and blurry around the edges, like she was seeing everything through a pool of seawater. There was a painful pounding in her head and blood thundering in her ears. Her navy colored skirt, which earlier had been billowing in the wind with the echoes of her family's laughter, was now limp and cold against her bare legs. Her whole body felt numb with occasional waves of needle-like pain and she was unable to move. However, these sensations were falling into a blank space.

No sound, no sight except piercing white, and no feeling. It felt relaxing to fall into this peaceful place. At other times, she would have been filled with enormous terror, but because of the place she was in, it was like going to bed after a long day. As she was climbing into the white she felt a sensation of hands on her body, but it was soft and faint as tendrils of fog. She felt a change of air wrapping around her body, but not her mind. She had finished climbing the base of the white, calm area, and climbed the first steps of a tall, white staircase. She felt something stiff, cold, and damp beneath her in the real world, but it was far away. She looked up the staircase with a sense of relief: she was almost to the top.

In the real world, she felt straps pull across her body and something tightened to her face, but it all had the sensation of a feather. She stopped her ascendance to the top and froze.

Abruptly, she was dragged into her real body and out of her mind. The sounds of sudden shouts, sirens, and pounding feet blared in her ears like giant waves.

It was dark out, but red and blue beams of light pulsed in the darkness. She could now clearly feel the gash on her arm and the miniature but painful cuts on her face, chest, and hands. Her legs felt as if a raging fire was burning the outside and inside of them. She screamed at the pain although no sound emerged from her open throat. Tears left her eyes, leaving glassy streaks against her cheek and running down her neck. Her body spasmed uncontrollably and the sobs in her chest seemed to rip her insides apart. Thrashing, she realized straps attached on her forehead, shoulders, and legs forced her to stay on a hard backboard, and a breathing mask smashed against her face made her feel like she was suffocating.

Moving wildly she managed to loosen the bond on her head and smacked the mask against her shoulder, pushing it off. The white area almost drowned her instantly. She felt someone reattach the wretched mask, the small strings burning above her ears.

She was stuck. She felt dizzy and sick. Thinking felt like walking in a maze of mirrors. Only when it had finally seized her fully, did she realize she was going into the dark space of unconsciousness as it pulled her in forcefully with no mercy or comfort.

And unlike the white mind-space she had been in earlier, she felt everything.

Orange Ribbon

ear a cliff's edge in Black Bull, England, stands a pale, two story yellow house. It wasn't the house itself that was significant, it was rather the mother and daughter living inside. It wasn't a happy household. With just the two living all alone together there were constant fights. The husband and father of the household (who usually prevented these fights) had died three years previous when his daughter, Alice, was just 7 years old. The mother and widow of the household was a woman in her early thirties named Alexis. Alexis was a person who was soured by life's events and constantly felt that the world had wronged her. Her daughter Alice had once thought that the world was perfect with no need to improve, but now having witnessed—and witnessing still—her mom's dreadful outbursts and harsh demeanor, she thought otherwise.

Alice, who had loved her father dearly, was crushed after his death. To keep herself out of a constant state of misery like her mother, she started involving herself in the fascinating world of genetics and space. She quickly lost interest in genotypes and phenotypes and focused on the spacious world of stars, moons, and black holes. By age 8 Alice had decided that she wanted to be an astronaut. But Alexis was angered by her daughter, ridiculed her, and claimed in fits of resentment that Alice had hated her father and had been happy that he died. Alice, stung by Alexis' claims, quickly cut their daughter-mother bond, leaving them both with no friend to help them through their grief. By the time Alice was 10 she was wholly immersed in the void of space and Alexis had turned to abusive behavior.

I breathe in the scent of salty early morning air, listen

to the shrieks of seagulls and pelicans, and feel the cold dewy grass beneath my dark feet. Alexis has already woken up. I can tell because I hear sounds of glass shattering and the groan of the house's frame as it shakes from stomping feet. I tried in the beginning to understand her, but then I decided I didn't care. If she didn't care for me, I wouldn't care for her. I run my hands over my long bushy hair; Alexis has neglected cutting it. I pull out the kitchen scissors that I had put in my coat and use them to cut the hair to my chin. Bushy clumps of hair lay on the ground around me, making a dark halo around my feet.

"ALICE!" I hear Alexis shriek.

Letting out a shaky breath I hide my hand holding the scissors in my coat pocket, then pad to the back door, opening it with care, making sure not to make noise. I go to the kitchen where I know Alexis will be waiting. I find her standing on top of the dining table swatting at flies with an empty takeout box, surrounded by dirty dishes as mice scurry for safety.

"I'm here," I say, making sure my voice doesn't quiver. She turns around, glaring scornfully at where I stand.

"Where is MY bottle! I know you took it, you

filthy piece of trash!" she spits out wrathfully.

Struggling to breathe evenly through the spasms in my diaphragm I level my eyes at her dingy slipper-clad feet.

"I never touched your stupid spirits," I croak lamely.

"Oh really?" she hisses menacingly, jumping down from the table, and throwing the empty carton at me. I cringe as the box's sharp corner jabs me beside my eye. Alexis stomps across the splintered floor and grabs my face, digging her fingers into my soft skin, then slams me against the wall and proceeds to kick me. "TELL ME WHERE MY BOTTLE IS!" she screams in anger, her eyes flaring with hatred.

"I don't know!" I wail, covering my head.

The kicking abruptly stops as Alexis stares down at me. Then, letting out a savage smirk, she flounces upstairs to my room.

"NO!" I shriek, grabbing her arm and pulling at it to prevent her from going to my hideout.

She turns around, slapping me sharply across my right cheek before sprinting up the steps.

"NO! STOP! IT'S MY STUFF! LEAVE IT ALONE!" I cry, stumbling after her.

Upstairs I can hear a door banging open and loud crashes. I run into my room and let out a gasp. Inside, Alexis has already broken my makeshift telescope and my solar system diagram and is tearing apart the space books I stole from the school library.

"STOP!" I sob, ripping the remaining books from her arms.

Ignoring me she grabs Leo, a stuffed animal lion that Dad gave to me when I was 4, and throws it out the window.

"LEO!" I call out with a grimace on my face.

"Where is my bottle?" Alexis asks, grabbing my lamp, ripping the cord out of the outlet and raising it above my head.

Whimpering, I drop the books and pull the scissors out, pointing them at her.

Letting out a raspy laugh she brings the lamp down on my hands. I shudder as the scissors fly out of my grip and the lamp leaves a bruise.

"It's in the bathroom cabinet," I blurt out.

Alexis smiles darkly and walks loudly to the bathroom to get her alcohol, only stopping to spit on my face.

I curl up under my bed, watching the dust bunnies and cockroaches go by. I had always thought that bad things happened just because they do, but lately I've wondered if they happen for a reason. What did I do to lose my father and my childhood? What did I do to earn beatings from Alexis every day? Is it because I lied about eating my classmates' snacks in preschool? Was it the time I ignored the new kid? Was it not telling my father I loved him every day? Or not apologizing to my mother for not putting my dishes in the sink? I wish I knew so I could set it right.

I wait until my breath has evened out and my heart beats in rhythm to sneak downstairs and outside to retrieve a damp Leo. Leo is my most treasured possession. I used to have multiple comforts in my room, but Alexis either burnt or sold them.

I still remember getting Leo. Six years ago in music class we were singing about Eleanor the elephant, Bailey the bear, and Leo the lion. I remember Mrs. Bumble telling me Happy Birthday and asking me what present I wanted. "A LION!" I squealed. I remember getting home that day and seeing my dad holding a stuffed animal lion that had a sticker on its chest that said: 'Hello, my name is Leo.' I remember crying happily while also hugging my dad and trying to kiss my new toy on the head. I even remember seeing Alexis smile. I used to have a picture of that day but after Father died, Alexis grabbed all the pictures of him from around the house and flushed them down the toilet. After that she had grabbed all of his belongings and had thrown them over the side of the cliff into the frigid foamy water below.

Alexis hates staying in the house. She spends as little time as possible inside its walls. Our house has few things within. I have been lucky enough to stay in school. People mock me and spread unpleasant gossip but it's safer there than it is here.

When I finally hear the buzz of Alexis' bike, I go inside to get ready for school. Placing Leo in my backpack, I pull off my shabby nightgown and put on an excited yellow shirt with a cartoon axolotl, leggings with various rows of multi-colored stripes, and cheap plastic earrings. All from the second hand store. Grabbing my neon pink backpack, I head out the door. It usually takes fifteen minutes to walk to school, but I always leave the house a few hours earlier.

I walk slowly, looking at the poppies at the side of the road, drooping at the weight of the dust on their petals. Stooping down, I wipe the dirt off of their red blades. Freed of the weight they pop up joyfully, facing their heads to the sun. I look at them wondering what it would be like to be a flower. I fold my feet beneath me like a seat, and stroke the poppies flimsy-looking stems and leaves. I lean over them, tasting their tart, spicy scent.

This is my favorite time of the day—watching the sun rise high over the breathing ocean and being alone listening to the swallows and bees; watching the flowers and clovers toss their crowns with the breeze. Straightening up, I continue walking down the broken sidewalk. "Step on a crack, break your mother's back; step on a line, break your father's spine." I mummer to myself and hop viciously upon every crack I can see and jump over every line while saying a whispered, "I love you."

A couple of hours later I arrive at the school. I'm a few minutes early so I sit by the gate watching some ants collecting doughnut crumbs. They hurry around like they're about to be late for ant class. There is one ant I am very fond of. She runs around dragging a piece of colorful orange ribbon. I name her Turmeric like her ribbon. The ant chasing after her I name Jude the Rude because he keeps trying to steal her treasure. I imagine being Turmeric and telling Jude the Rude to grab his OWN ribbon. Suddenly, a glamorous green beetle scuttles over my toes, wriggles underneath the school fence, pinches Turmeric between its pincers, and eats her. I watch as Jude the Rude grabs the orange ribbon and starts dragging it away in a frantic state. The beetle ignores him and sits contentedly upon the asphalt. Seething inwardly, I pull out my pencil and crush the great ugly green beetle with its eraser. Nearby I hear a gasp. I look up, glaring.

"Beetle killerrrrr!!!" one of the girls moans dramatically, pressing the back of her hand to her forehead, pretending to be faint.

"Oh? Did you name it?! What was its name? Ursula?! Hades?!" I retort, standing up, one hand on my hip, the other wielding the pencil.

"No, that's your name!" sneers the leader of the group, gripping her Hello Kitty skirt in her hands.

"I said two names, dummy!" I scream at them.

"Well then you're like both of them!" they shout back.

"AM NOT!" I roar.

"YOU'RE LIKE EVERY EVIL PERSON IN THE DISNEY MOVIES!!" they yell before stomping away, their tight braids swaying.

I watch as the five girls strut away, giggling about some joke while swinging their sequin backpacks in their hands. Turning away, I smash Jude the Rude and the rest of the pathetic anthill then stomp away to Mr. Smith's classroom.

Pushing past Mr. Smith himself, I walk into the dull room. The walls are grayish wood that has seen too many years, and the chalkboard in the front is smeared from all the inappropriate jokes that have been rubbed off. The chairs are a cheap gray plastic and tables are made from wood pulp compressed together, painted a painful yellow and covered with a sticky see-through plastic finish.

"Hello Alice," says Mr. Smith in his gravelly voice.

"Hello," I grumble, sliding into my chair. Instead of peppering me with questions and asking if I was all right like any other teacher would, Mr. Smith pulls out some paper and markers.

"Art contest?" he challenges, raising his thick eyebrows. Grinning, I pull a second chair to my table and bounce into my seat in excitement.

Mr. Smith sits in the chair across from me and lays a piece of paper and a handful of faded markers in front of me.

"Two minutes, starting now," Mr. Smith proclaims, starting on his drawing.

Determined not to be beaten, I furiously scribble across the paper with a black marker. Mr. Smith draws in a calmer manner, humming a lullaby underneath his breath. I huff, exasperated as I switch between my limited colors: purple, green, pink, orange, and black. The forms of three people pop into existence on my page.

"One minute left," Mr. Smith announces, glancing at his stopwatch.

I quickly draw some dirt with grass on top and an orange colored sun in the top left corner.

"Can we use stamps?" I ask, raising my head.

Mr. Smith nods, smiling encouragingly.

I get up and search for the perfect stamp. With satisfaction, I find a grim reaper stamp. Rushing to my drawing, I stamp the image onto my paper. The stopwatch vibrates. I slide my picture to Mr. Smith in triumph, while he slides his own art to me. I look at Mr. Smiths picture. It's a mushroom with a red cap, white spots, surrounded by emerald grass and a simple smile. "Can I keep this?" I plead, holding the drawing to my heart.

"Yes," says Mr. Smith before looking at my picture. He frowns. "Is that an arrow in his chest?" Mr. Smith asks, pointing to the dead guy in the drawing.

"Yes. Alexis murdered him," I reply, pointing to the woman who is smiling and holding a bow.

Mr. Smith clears his throat loudly. "So, your mom is the one holding the bow?"

"Yes. It's Alexis."

"And is the dead guy your dad?"

"Uh huh, Alexis killed Dad," I say, pointing to the arrow in his chest.

"Is that you?" Mr. Smith asks, clearly bemused and pointing to the girl wearing a crown.

"Yes. And that's the grim reaper coming to take Daddy's soul," I explain, pointing to the stamp mark.

"Why do you and your dad have purple skin?"

"I didn't have a light brown marker."

"And your mom is orange?"

"Everyone draws white people with orange. That's why I drew Alexis that color."

"No. White people are drawn with the color peach. Kind of like orange but lighter."

"OOOOHH. That makes more sense." I mutter, tilting my head as the school bell rings.

"Class is about to start, Alice. Get ready," says Mr. Smith, getting up and putting my drawing on his desk.

I pull my backpack into my lap and carefully place Mr. Smith's signed picture inside.

I sit rigidly in my seat, backpack in my lap. Mr. Smith paces the front of the classroom. "Today during writing we will be heading down to Mrs. Belt-Bushes first grade class to partner with the kids there. For the next two weeks we will be writing a story with your selected partners. No inappropriate or foul language, no rude words or bullying." Mr. Smith tells the room.

"What can we write about?" asks one boy without raising his hand.

"Nothing scary or bad. Otherwise, you have free rein. And remember it's not just you writing your story, it's you AND your partner," Mr. Smith replies. "We also have a new student that will be coming to our classroom soon. Remember to treat them with respect and kindness."

An excited atmosphere fills the room, the other

students chatter in anticipation. I sulk, knowing that another student will mean I will have another tormenter. I pull a marker out of my backpack and start doodling on my desktop. We have to wait a couple minutes before the new kid comes.

When she finally opens the door we are all awestruck. She has wavy yellow hair that reaches past her elbows, wide, very pale, blue eyes, fair skin, and a face covered in light brown freckles. That was what I noticed. Everyone else noted her expensive tie-dye shirt, shiny purple skirt, and her elaborately crafted backpack and headband. Mr. Smith smiles politely and waves her to the front of the class. "Can you tell us your name?" he asks.

The girl starts speaking in a strong, uplifting voice, "My name is Lexi Brooks. I'm 10 years old and from Canada." She levels a severe look at all of us as if challenging us to tease her. I hate this girl who was stronger than me for having hair like the wheat that supported life, for having a better life than me. I glare at her wrathfully, my teeth clenched. That was the moment that she happened to see me. Instead of looking confused like I thought she would, she just gave me a sneer. Loathing flares through me as I go back to doodling on my desk.

After the new girl's arrival we have writing class in Mrs. Belt-Bushes' class. While everyone chose a partner I stay with Mr. Smith, saying I wouldn't participate if he wasn't my partner. Then, mercifully, we are released for recess.

Walking as far away from the other kids as I can, I go to the fence where the anthill is. The ants had opened the hill again and were dragging the beetle corpse to their home. Ignoring them, I grab the abandoned orange ribbon and pocket it in my worn coat.

"What are you doing?" came a scolding voice behind.

Ignoring the person, I walk away, proud when an outraged gasp comes from behind me. The new girl walks in front of me, hands on her hips, feet spread apart. "What are you doing?" she repeats angrily.

"Why do you want to know?" I retort, glowering right back at her.

"Because you appear to be a jerk and everyone avoids you. Is it because you're Black?" she says in a bossy voice.

"My skin is brown, you idiot," I snap, ignoring her question.

She smirks, tossing her head.

"Go away," I snarl, pushing her to the ground. Then I stomp back towards the school building.

Lexi cuts in front of me again.

"I asked what you were doing because you seemed sad. Talking helps people," she spits out.

I pause, startled at the unexpected words, but am quickly overcome with jealousy. "I am not SAD! I am HAPPY! And if I WAS SAD it would be because we live in a STUPID world! But of course YOU'RE fine! YOU probably have a BRILLIANT life!!" I say to her viciously.

She looks at me, frowning, appearing perplexed. "Do you want to play with me?"

"No."

"Why not?"

"No," I repeat, walking back to Mr. Smith's classroom. The school bell rings.

After seven brutal hours of school, bullying, and more book theft, I prepare to walk home. Hitching my backpack, heavy with new space books, I leave the building. However, when my foot hits the sidewalk I hear someone calling my name. Looking back in confusion I see the new girl, Lexi, holding a tall man's hand and waving to me. I hesitate. Grown-ups observe more than kids. If I were to ignore them, the man would think something was wrong. I sigh in remorse, walking over to the pair.

"Hello Alice!" Lexi says brightly.

"Hello," I say politely, looking her square in the face. She looks smug.

"Me and my dad were wondering if you wanted us to drive you home." Lexi says, gesturing to the smiling man beside her.

I frown and shake my head. "I'll just walk home."

"Please?"

"My house is close by."

"We don't mind driving you home," Lexi begs, her hands clasped in front of her.

The man finally intervenes. "It would be our pleasure to drive you home."

I sigh inwardly before nodding. "Okay," I say.

Smiling the duo leads me to their fancy looking Subaru.

Muttering curses to myself, I slide in the backseat.

"Where do you live?" Lexi's dad asks.

"On the outskirts of town, close by the cliffs," I mumble, sliding lower into my seat.

"Ooh! Can you do cliff diving here?" Lexi pipes up.

"Probably."

We sit in silence for twenty minutes.

"Is that your house?" Mr. Brooks exclaims, pointing to a building in the distance.

Squinting my eyes I look to where he points. "Yes. I could get out here."

Shaking his head, he drives up to the front of the swaying house. I quickly scramble out of the car, wave to them, and bound inside.

The next two months turned out more glorious than I could have imagined. Me and Lexi quickly became friends and spent multiple nights and days at her house. Lexi is obsessed with flowers and wants to be a botanist. She was thrilled when I said I wanted to be an astronaut. "So much to explore."

My grades had skyrocketed when Lexi told me I had to have good grades to be an astronaut. Lexi, like me, loved Mr. Smith, and joined our morning art contests, and also like me had an intense dislike for the other children. "They're so snooty," she had said, wrinkling her nose after she had witnessed one of their bullying periods.

"You learn to live with it," I had replied, shrugging and grinning at her. We only ever played with them if our game required more than two people.

Lexi's dad, I learned, was smart and generous, giving us pie for lunch and little comic strips tucked in our lunch boxes that he got us. He also had asked if I wanted to stay in their house after he witnessed the condition of our house and had guessed that Alexis was an alcoholic. I had moved my limited prized possessions to Lexi's room and shared her bed with her like we were sisters. I also returned all the library books I stole. It was the happiest I had been in a long time.

"What should we do today?" I ask, pulling on purple jeans.

"Can't do anything today," Lexi grumbles, rubbing the bruises on her arms. "I have to go to the doctor."

I look up, pulling my backpack over my shoulder. "Didn't you go three weeks ago?" I ask, narrowing my eyes.

"I did, but Daddy's been really weird and is making me go again."

"Why?"

"I have no idea."

"None?"

"Nope," she replies before letting out a hacking cough.

I look at Lexi closely. Her skin is paler than usual, her tired eyes drooping, and her body skinny like a dead twig.

"You do look sick," I admit, looking away and thinking of all the days she had to stay home because of colds, fevers, and violent coughing fits.

She dismisses this with a snort. "It's fall, everyone's getting sick."

I listen to the voice of Wesley Shultz, lead singer of the Lumineers, sing "In the Light" through the living room Alexa.

"Lexi, where's your mom?" I ask Lexi who is wrapped up in a blanket and nibbling saltine crackers.

"Dead. She got really sick and died when I was 6," she answers, rubbing her thinning hair and taking wheezing breaths.

Later I was told by Mr. Brooks that I had to go back home with all of my stuff, and I did, holding back betrayed tears. I didn't find relief at school either because Lexi wasn't there, rumor was she was staying overnight at hospitals.

I tried visiting Lexi four times. The first three attempts, Mr. Brooks answered the door and sent me on my way. The fourth time its was Lexi who answered, or more a shadow of the old Lexi. She looked deathly pale from what I saw of her face. "What's wrong?" I had asked, reaching for her hands. She recoiled, then letting out a sob she pulled back the hood of the sweatshirt and pulled up the sleeves. This time I recoiled. Her head was bald, not a golden-yellow hair in sight, and her arms were a patchwork of black bruises and deep red rashes.

"I'm sick, I'm sick like mom!" she sobbed, reaching for me. Then Mr. Brooks hands reached from the depths of the house and pulled crying Lexi back into its walls. He gave me a look that told me I should be ashamed of myself. For whatever reason, I don't know. I do know he's trying to keep me from seeing Lexi, My Best Friend.

I sneak past Alexis who is slumped against the grimy table. I clutch the envelope holding a short, happy message for Lexi. As soon as I step out into the December day the wind bites me with a ferocious nip. Shivering, I push through the ankle-deep snow. The moon hangs in the sky like it didn't want to sink beneath the horizon and go to sleep. It takes some extra time to trudge to Lexi's house and then school but I do it. The envelope is safely delivered. Damp and freezing I step into Mr. Smith's toasty classroom.

"Have you heard from Lexi lately?" I ask, my jaw aching.

No," says Mr. Smith, giving me a weird look.

"Art contest?" I whisper, holding up a piece of paper, my eyes to the floor.

Again Mr. Smith gives me the look. "What about after school?" he says in a voice that settled it.

Nodding faintly, my nose bright red, I sit in my assigned chair, the one next to Lexi's. The day is gray and slow, every hour inching by like a snail. I feel cold and empty, though I didn't know exactly why. Inside my pocket I clench the faded orange ribbon. After the school day is over I approach Mr. Smith. He places a piece of paper in front of me. "Any color and words allowed," he mutters.

I carefully pick a deep orange and draw a pretty silk ribbon with an ant pulling it and another ant who seems rude but is actually playing a game with the other ant. They are standing near the anthill they worked so hard to build. Nearby, a beetle peers at the two with slit eyes and a foot looms above.

"Time's up," Mr. Smith whispers, swapping papers. "What's this?" he asked, holding the picture up.

"Something I saw the day I met Lexi," I say boldly. He just nods weakly, pointing to the paper in my hands. Looking down all I see is the bold word **CANCER** and caricature of Lexi's face beneath.

"What's this?" I remark in confusion.

"Do you know what cancer is?" Mr. Smith replies.

"No."

"It's a sickness that can kill people if not treated right."

"Why is Lexi's face on here?"

"Lexi had cancer."

"She doesn't anymore?"

"Alice...."

"What?"

"Lexi is gone. She's dead." Mr. Smith gulps, running his hands through his hair. "She had a very severe case of cancer called leukemia." He lets out a sad hiccup.

I stare at him then let out a delirious laugh and run out of the room.

"Alice," I hear him moan sadly.

Ignoring him, I run out of the school to Lexi's house. My vision is grainy and I trip and fall multiple times. I pound on the pale blue door until my hands are sore. "Lexi! Lexi!" I wail.

The door swings open. It's Mr. Brooks holding a bottle of alcohol, his breath smelling sharp and musty.

"What...?" he says, his words slurred. He leans heavily against the frame.

"Where's Lexi?!!" I snap.

"Not here. She left me. They both did." His sad gray eyes droop, the flesh on his face bright red.

He's a coward. He's a sissy that has no will power. He's just like Alexis.

I run home without taking a single break. Adrenaline burns my body, my veins throb and my eyes blur. I stop once I reach the house and walk slowly to the cliff. I let out a bloodcurdling scream, my chest bursts into painful flames of hatred and tears streak down my face and freeze, pinching the tender flesh beneath. I raise my voice until my head feels like it will pop off, and then jump over the craggily cliff into the dense black water below. I feel the wind scream in my ears and pound against my body. I feel my body smash onto the water like concrete. And then everything bursts into white.

Banished

Archibald stares curiously at the sleeping teenagers laying among the ferns and moss. "Hello," he whispers, nudging them with his booted foot. The girl mutters angrily in her sleep and the boy stays as he had been before. "Hello," Archibald tries again, crouching next to them. Nothing. Then, as quick as a boar, the girl slams her head into his chest, knocking the breath out of him and sending him sprawling onto the ground.

"Nice," says a throaty male voice nearby.

"Were you both already awake?" asks Archibald, wheezing and struggling to his feet.

"Yup," comes the replies from his traveling partners. Then they are off again

Archibald met them both when he was exploring around the Emerald Mountains. Both had roots of pitch black hair and both had been banished from their tribe. When he had innocently asked why, the girl punched him in the face and the other just shrugged his shoulders.

The goddess-like girl was named Rosemary and the boy named Thyme.

(In his opinion, Thyme was a very cliché name.)

Archibald learned that, unfortunately, Rosemary had feelings for Thyme and vice versa. They hadn't told Archibald that he could come with them, but they hadn't stopped him either. They traveled frequently to other surrounding villages and traded the hides and meat from their travels. Each moon the two hired someone to bring food and money to a village that he had never heard of.

Rosemary called him Balladeer, and when Archibald asked why she complained that his nighttime ballads kept her awake.

After that, he stopped his nighttime ritual, but the nickname stuck. He had daydreams of Thyme dying and Rosemary weeping into his shoulder, telling him how she loved him only. Of course he never wished anyone in the party to die, but the fantasy passed the time.

Archibald learned that he and Rosemary were both 15 summers old while Thyme was 17 summers old. After a year had passed he asked again why they had been banished from their tribe and to his surprise this time they answered.

"Because we stole food from the village to feed our families," Rosemary recounted bitterly.

"How did you meet?" Archibald inquired, leaning forward.

"We've been together our entire lives," Thyme answered, chewing on a piece of charred venison.

"At the end they called us the thieving cousins."

"Because you stole together?" he asked.

Rosemary looked at him impatiently, "No, because we're cousins."

Archibald took this in shock, his mouth gaping open. "But you love each other."

"Yes," replied Rosemary. "As family." Then, getting up, she washed her hands in a nearby creek.

"Are you sending food and money to your family?" he asked.

"Yes, we hire someone every moon to deliver food and money," Thyme replied, giving him an amused grin.

Archibald smiled ear to ear and got up as the trio once again moved on to explore more places.

The Oregon Trail

March 24th - April 9th, 1842

LEAVING FOR THE JOURNEY

W

e are going to California. Papa says it would be best for Ma and Lu. They caught measles last winter and never recovered. I do believe Papa hopes fresh air will heal them, but me and Theodore believe otherwise. No matter how I weep, Papa refuses to hear me out. Says he "got to help his ladies." Guess I'm more of a scrawny girl to him.

The packing started today. Papa says we're leaving for warmer weather and a better home. We purchased a prairie schooner and started filling it with bacon and lard. Ma lamented over grandma's rug while Lu fainted at the dread of leaving her beloved Ross behind. Papa spanked Theodor and me whenever we made a protest of some sort. Who knew a belt could hurt so?

My biggest fear is we will be traveling with our drunk Uncle Ted and an abundance of strangers. Plus we have mules instead of steed or oxen. I do not know if we will survive this six month journey.

Papa has seeked advice for the travel and since little has traveled our destined path little advice is to be given:

1. Natives steal horses.

2. Wide rivers are to be avoided because they pose great danger.

3. Although prone to stealing horses, Natives are a needed help on the trail.

The boy next door, Wyne, heard of our soon leaving and gave me a beautiful blue rose.

With love and affection, Leigh Smith

April 10th- October 3rd, 1842: THE TRAIL

I have to write briefly for paper is scarce.

Leaving Missouri is harder than anticipated. It is around 2,000 miles of harsh weather to our destination and Lu is moaning like a pathetic, stupid toad.

I have not written in so long! I am delighted about some previous events. I wrote on Independence Rock!! It took great effort and one of Theodor's knives. He wasn't pleased. Then we visited the Whitman Mission! We ate till our stomachs were full. The Natives were friendly and good traders unlike those at Independence Rock. Papa seeks more advice. That is all for tonight.

Lu is dead, Theodor and Papa are ill and we had to leave Ma behind because she went insane from Typhoid.

Lu, Papa and most likely Ma are all dead. Theodor's better but one of the mules kicked me yesterday and I cannot walk without a limp.

Found Papa's advice paper. Three more added entries.

4. Hunt for extra food.
5. Keep the wagon in condition for travel. A broken wagon is dangerous.

6. *It is recommended to travel in groups.*

With sorrow and regret, Leigh Smith

October 3rd, 1842 - Date lost: AT AN END

Me and Theodor, and miraculously Uncle Ted, have ar-rived in the golden wheat fields of California. Half of the group died during the horrid trip. It's splendid here but hardly worth the trip. Also Uncle Ted spent all of the money on alcohol, so we are bankrupt.

Theodor is once more sick and cannot build a house and I can hardly walk from exhaustion. Uncle Ted lost us the first chance he got, stealing our remaining goods.

Money, a manmade disaster. Theodor and Me started arguing about how to make a living in which he suggested I be a maid. Then I retorted by remarking him being a slave. He finished the small talk by calling me a dirty native and stomped off to the swift river. Later, the neighbors told me they had found Theodor's drowned body. I called upon Uncle Ted by mail and all he had to say about the matter was that I was a stupid girl. Some people may differ from me, but I believe this Oregon trail is a path to punish Us for all of our sins and greed.

With everlasting sadness, Leigh Smith

Papa's advice paper:

7. Drink cider to reserve water.
8. Recommended to walk 12 to 15 miles a day.
9. Storytelling passes time.

John Smith, 1802-1842 _Food poisoning

Mary Smith, 1808-1842 _Typhoid

Theodor Smith, 1824-1842_Drowned

Lu Smith, 1825-1842 _Cholera

Leigh Smith, 1828-1843_Suicide

Homeless

ia tucked her ears into the hood of her pink sweatshirt and watched her little brother Matz play with his worn teddy bear. Around her she could hear echoing footsteps and loud voices meld together into an indiscernible background noise. Nervously, she wished that her mother would hurry back from the store. From the corner of her eye, she saw a tall old man with a scraggly beard stop and watch her and her brother. Mia turned so she faced the grandpa and bared her teeth defensively. The old man smiled back coldly then walked toward a mat on the other end of the homeless shelter.

Mia's shoulders loosened a little bit as she turned back toward Matz who was sleepily laying his head on his teddy bear. Mia lifted her brother and placed him on their solitary green mat. Yawning, he curled up, clutching his stuffed animal, and quickly fell asleep. Sitting down, Mia looked at their shopping cart that held dingy blankets, a couple of blue tarps, battered water bottles, and other stuff—some valuable, some useless. Reaching into her pocket, she pulled out a fidget spinner, a toy from the small homeless gift bags that some people gave out in Seattle. She spun the toy, listening to its pleasant hum as she waited for her mother to come back. Nearby, she heard the tap of high heels. She got up eagerly and stood on her tiptoes, looking for her mother over the turmoil of dirty bodies and trash.

Her mother strode toward their spot—her dyed curls swinging over her bare shoulders. Mia admired how strong her mother seemed in her green crop-top, tight black skirt, dirty cream-colored heels, and her cheap sunglasses perched on her head.

"Hi, Mia," said her mother as she strode up to her, a shopping bag swinging from her arm. "You didn't give anything away this time I hope?"

Mia shook her head, rocking on her heels. "I didn't give anything away. Promise."

"Good. It's hard enough to watch you and John without you both giving out stuff to every passing stranger," her mother said in disgust, her beautiful raspy voice almost angry.

Feeling small, Mia hunched her shoulders. "It's Matthew, not John, Mommy."

Her mother stopped just as she was walking toward the shopping cart and came back toward her. "Amelia Nakusa Fernsby, I know your brother's name! It's a good thing you're such a cutie or I would be angry," she said, painfully pinching Mia's cheek. Then she turned around and threw the shopping bag into the cart.

Rubbing her face where her mom had pinched it, Mia sat down on the mat next to Matthew.

"Could you play with my hair, Mia? I walked around all day looking for food for your brother," said her mother, kneeling before Mia.

"Sure," Mia said, grabbing a brush and curlers from a plastic bag in the cart.

Mia waited for her mother to sit down before gently brushing her hair. Her mother loved dyeing her hair. Last month it was dark purple now it was vibrant artificial red. Mia brushed her mother's hair until all the waves were gone and started rolling the hair in curlers.

"Make sure it's close to the scalp," her mother said, rubbing off her makeup and checking her progress in a small hand mirror.

Mia hummed to herself as she did her mother's hair. "Mommy, when can we have a house and beds?" she asked, putting the last of the red hair in a pink curler.

"Mia, I have things to worry about. Momma is busy." Her mother rubbed the last of her lipstick off.

Mia licked her lips as she played with the brush, "What about your momma and poppa? Can we stay with them?"

Her mother whirled around, aghast. "No! Your grandma and grandpa are devils of Satan himself! I even saw their horns and forked tails once! You have to pray that somebody drops a piano on their heads before they hurt anyone else like they did me! See, they gave me this scar! They're awful!" her mother ranted, passionately showing Mia a scar on her arm.

Mia rubbed her face in confusion. "You said Daddy gave you that when he attacked you with a knife."

"No, your wicked grandparents did. And I said no such thing, you ungrateful wretch. I knew you and your brother would be horrible, stupid children. That's why your middle name is Nakusa and your brother's is Amasa. You both hate me!" sobbed her mother, throwing her mirror on the ground, denting the back and making spider web fractures on the glass.

Mia backed away and cuddled up against her brother, knowing her mom's fit would go as fast as it came, like it usually did.

Mia knew for a fact that her mother's scar came from her dad, she had been there when it had happened. Her dad had been abusive to her and her mother and had ignored her brother's existence. He also drank excessively and sold weed. Maybe he still did. Mia had not seen her dad in two years, when she was 7 and her brother had been 3. And she hadn't seen her grandparents since she was 5. Matthew had been a year old and her mother had taken both of them to see Momma and Poppa. They both had white hair and soft wrinkly faces with kind eyes and smiles. During the visit, when her mother went out shopping with Matthew, she asked her grandparents what was wrong with her mom. She already knew her dad drank too much, but her mother was a mystery. Her mother would say she saw something that wasn't there, said violent and unexpected things, had sudden mood swings, and did irresponsible things. Yet she denied all this.

Her grandparents had answered her question, confirming that her mom's problems weren't her imagination. "Your mom has schizophrenia, hon," said her grandma in a sad, creaky voice. "It's an illness that makes your mom sad and makes her do strange things."

Mia vividly remembered asking if anyone could help her mommy.

"Yes, but she won't allow them to help, and she doesn't take the medicine to make her better," her grandpa had answered.

At age 9, she was already homeless, and it was entirely her parents' fault.

Cats and Colors

There was once a time when cats were all white. Some had different hair lengths, bodies, and faces, but all the cats had the same pearly white coats.

One day, the cats had an art contest to see who had the best paintings (no one won, for cats are horrific at art). When no one won, the cats flew into a fury and started throwing paint of many colors at one another. Except for bright unnatural colors, cats prefer colors they are used to seeing in the wild. After the cats had exhausted themselves and lay panting on the ground they noticed the state of their fur. Grumbling in distress, they went to a nearby river to clean their coats. They did not lick themselves because paint is bitter and thick. But when they dunked their fur into the river, the paint did not come out. Vigorously they scrubbed the paint and still it would not come out.

Some cats, in their frustration, dropped their coats in the water and the river swept them away. Others, unable to clean the paint out, put their furs back on and walked home in their new stripes and colors. The cats who lost their coats trembled in the cold while the other white cats who had not joined in the painting were as pearly as they ever were.

And that is why we have Persian, Rag-doll, Tabbies, Siamese, Sphynx, and many more varieties of cats.

Heirloom

"Hello sir, would you like an apple juice, ginger ale, or Pepsi?" asked the stewardess, giving the old man a cheeky smile. The elderly man gave her an angry glare before demanding a Coke. The stewardess tossed her mousy curls giving him a sour look, then grabbed a chilled Pepsi from the cart and slammed it on his tray.

She marched down the aisle proudly, her heels clicking against the floor. Pushing the cart into its compartment she sat in a seat in the back of the plane. She pulled out a thick notebook and a flashy silver pen. Her pale fingers traced the cream colored paper and wrote in blue ink some interesting characters she had encountered that day: a woman who was an acclaimed scientist, a young boy helping his father expand his business, and a handsome man pursuing the art of acting who no doubt would succeed with that stunning smile of his. Smirking, she fingered the curvy handwriting with delight.

From around her throat she lifted a necklace with blackened links; at the end was a flat piece of hammered metal homing a large emerald, tiny topaz pieces, and small golden flowers. The necklace seemed to swallow the light around it, turning everything dim and gray. Gently, she removed the necklace and placed it into her purse. As soon as her fingers left the rusty links, the churning minds of those around her dissipated. Leaning back she gave a scathing look to the passengers on the plane, for none of them had a family heirloom like hers that allowed her to read the minds and lives of those around her. None of them had such a special treasure. And her job allowed her to see a lot of people in a single day.

However, the one thought that did not occur in her proud head, was that living in the lives of others had prevented her from living one of her own.

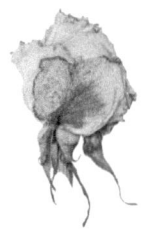

Cage

"**I**f you care a bit about these children," shrieked a female voice, "you will leave!"

"They're my children too, Alyssa," said a male quietly but seething with rage.

"No, Joseph. THEY ARE MINE," hissed Alyssa.

"Mommy?" said Heather, coming out from her hiding place behind the door.

"Get back in bed!!" screamed Joseph, swinging a murky bottle at her.

"Bu... but?" stammered Heather, stumbling back.

"OUT!!"

Heather stared at her dad through tears, then fled to her room. Sobbing on her bed, she wondered why her parents were always fighting. Bitterly hiding her head underneath her pillow, she imagined loving parents that never got drunk and never EVER hit them. She and her older siblings deserved that.

Tap. Tap tap tap came the sound of someone gently knocking the door with their knuckles.

"Yes?" Heather sniffled, lifting her head and wearing the pillow like an oversized hat.

"It's Rea and Pip. Can we come in?" whispered a feminine voice outside her room.

"Yes," moaned the young girl pitifully.

The door creaked open and two figures walked in. Rachel immediately strode over to her little sister and picked her up while her twin brother shut the door with a sharp click.

"Had a tough day, Hattie?" asked Philip while Rachel planted a kiss on her head.

"Some teachers at school called Daddy and Mommy drunkards. And Daddy yelled at me," said Heather with small hiccups.

"Shhh," he cautioned, glancing nervously toward the wall that separated them from their parents.

"Everybody has bad days, Hattie baby," cooed her sister, bouncing Heather on her hip.

"How long till I'm fifteen like you and Rea?" Heather asked her older brother in adoration.

"Seven years," Pip answered, holding up his fingers. Heather let out a small yawn. Sitting down on the bed, they tucked the littlest between the older two. Rea pulled out a small flashlight and softly read to Hattie while Pip hugged them tightly and looked around as if guarding them from the small dark room. From a small skylight, barely as big as a grate, the stars twinkled reassuringly. In the room next door they heard their parents fighting and smashing bottles. "Leave!" they heard Alyssa scream.

"Mommy…" said Heather as softly as the beat of moth wings.

"Shhhh," Pip whispered, giving his sister a gentle squeeze. He crawled out of the bed, putting Heather into his twin sister's lap. He walked carefully, opening the door so unfriendly orange light poured into the room.

Rachel stood up, putting Heather on her hip. "Philip, he's drunk," Rachel whispered. Heather buried her face into Rachel's shoulder.

"I know, but they'll hurt each other. Stay here," he whispered, kissing them both on top of the head.

He slipped silently out of the door, closing it. Heather's small fingers ran along the grainy wood of the frame. The voices they heard seemed blurry and muffled except for the shrill voice that called out in alarm. "WHAT DID YOU DO?!" they heard their mother exclaim.

Rachel yanked open the door and ran into the room where her mother was clutching her breast in terror. Laying on the ground was the young girls' cherished Pip, his nose bleeding and his neck twisted at a weird angle. Leaning over him was Joseph, standing lopsided, drinking from a bottle as if nothing was wrong.

"You drunk freak!" bellowed Rachel at her father, tears stinging her eyes and racing down her face. Heather cried a high songlike note of distress as she looked upon her beloved brother's still body.

Joseph looked up, a freakish smile twitching across his lips, his eyes clouded like a great storm. "More bloody children!" he announced in an angry garble. "GET OUT!" he yelled suddenly, stumbling towards them like a hunting lion. Rachel clutched Heather close to her, trembling, and bolted out the back door while Alyssa leaped upon her drunk husband in order to save her two remaining children.

Nightmare

He lay on the bed, staring at the dull plaster ceiling with distaste. It was March, the month his family always rented the pathetic house in the Cascades. As usual, his father did not come and his mother worked with ambition, even though the whole point of the trip was to relax. He didn't usually mind because Scout would always play with him. But this year he had left elementary school and entered the sixth grade. In middle school, the only things that mattered was who had the most girl-friends and who was the best at playing football. In middle school, the student rule was that playing was forbidden. And because he was trying to fit in, he followed the rules. Just then, his little sister bounced in, breaking his thought bubble.

"MAX!" she squealed in delight, "it's like a swimming pool outside!"

Glaring at his sister, Max stood up and peered out the window to prove her wrong—only to find she was right. He stood there in amazement. Even though the water was probably only two inches deep it covered every surface of the ground. This explained the weird sloshing, drumming sound. Max had just assumed his sister was taking a bath while also beating her toy drum. Rain screamed down from the gray sky, making the landscape a darker more gloomy color.

"Let's play!" Scout cried with unrepressed glee.

"No," he snapped. "This trip is for relaxing, not running around like a stupid kid." She paused long enough that he thought she was done.

"But you ARE a kid."

He furrowed his brow, put his hands on his hips, and thrust back his head. Scout considered this and decided her big brother must be sick.

"Hope you get better!" she said, trying to coo

kindly but sounding like a squeaky bird instead. Walking out briskly so she wouldn't get ill, she snapped the door shut.

Max twisted Scout's words the way pre-teens often do and thought she had just called him boring and mean. "I'LL SHOW YOU!" he yelled stupidly at the yellow door. He sat on the floor, moping like a dog without a cat to chase. Just when he was considering going to Mom and complaining that she was starving him and that she needed to give Scout to the orphanage for free, he heard a shrill scream. Peering out the warped glass of his window he saw a bat, a gigantic bat holding his thrashing sister. Or was it a bear? The creature had a tight pelt the color of rotting wood, a hunched back, and was standing on its muscular hind legs while its less impressive bony arms clutched Scout. It faced Max with its dark tear-shaped eyes, its face was entirely flat and sickle-like teeth stuck out from its maw. Opening its mouth, it imitated his sister's terrified and desperate screams. Gurgling in terror, Max ran to the door, locking it quickly, looking for something to block the door. But there were only two pieces of furniture (the bed and dresser, both a pale white) and his bulging black backpack. Standing there for two minutes he hyperventilated, waiting for the monster to get him, when he noticed that it was almost completely silent. There was no shouting. The sounds outside were quieter even though it was still pouring and he could hear his mom's keyboard clacking.

Undoing the simple lock he walked down the pale hallway into his mom's room. His mother was sitting there serenely staring at her screen. "Why are you not looking for Scout?" he asked simply.

"Because I'm working," his mom remarked harshly, turning in frustration towards him.

All Max noticed was that she looked like she was painted black and white before he walked out of the room. He ran around the house meaninglessly before standing in front of the door leading outside. Opening the door, he noted the onslaught outside raged harder than when he had looked out the window before. Taking a stuttering breath, he stepped off the top step and plunged ten feet deep into the tossing waves. Resurfacing from the frothy water, Max stared terrified at the changed landscape. The black sky bellowed above angrily and bullet hard rain pelted from above. The desolate house was being thrown around in the ocean's vengeful tides. And what once had been one hundred foot high trees of the Cascades, barely poked out of the seething water. Max screamed. Thunder clashed.

He paddled towards the floating house, and when he was within eight yards of it he had to watch in terror as it sank, creating a fast growing whirlpool. He made a sobbing choke before swimming rapidly to the tips of the trees. He reached the first tree when he slipped down the sloping water into the damp forest. Shuddering now from nerves and cold, he ventured forward, looking for Scout. While he trudged ahead he noticed the rain was softer and warmer. Because he was thirsty, Max closed his eyes, tilted his head back, and stuck out his tongue. When the first drops hit him he winced at the saltiness and wiped his tongue with his fingers. Pausing, he looked at his hands covered in blood. And looked at the blood raining from the sky. Shrieking, he ran forward, the forest a dim blur as he stumbled his way through. He tripped on a rock and fell to the floor in a mess. Looking up, tears streaking his face, he noticed Scout crouched, backing into a salmonberry bush, whimpering.

"SCOUT!" he shouted happily, but she disappeared into the bush without another sound. Standing up to go after her, Max heard her whimper again, this time from behind. Turning around, Max saw the monster, letting out mewing cries like Scout, as it sprung towards him, its maw encircling his head.

Max woke up before its spiked teeth bit down on his neck.

Hospital

He stared blankly at the muted TV, watching cartoon characters dance in the frame, waving their arms and doing cartwheels. Sighing with a mixture of bleakness and dread, he wiggled deeper into the folds of the thin blanket, wincing as he felt the IV pull in the crook of his arm. Taking deep shuddering breaths he turned his head the other way, trying to ignore the cold invasive needle. Instead, he focused on the blue diamond shapes on his white hospital outfit.

Claustrophobia kicked in as he glanced around

the small white room. Everything was white. Or light blue. Even the cartoon characters on the TV screen lacked bright inviting colors. Everything was cold. Trying to keep the panic at bay he tapped the tune of hot cross buns onto the metal rail of his bed. Instead of having a soothing effect, it let out tuneless bongs, making a sad funnel march. Was he going to die? What if he never had a dog? Or never saw his best friend again? What if he never saw his mom or dad again? Or his sister and brother? Did they hate him? Is that why they put him here?

Feeling nauseous, he swallowed his bitter tasting saliva. His throat felt like it was squeezing shut, like if he tried to swallow again he would choke to death.

He glanced at the clock on the wall. Roman numerals. He couldn't read Roman numerals.

He glanced around for a window before remembering there were none. He glanced at the blue tinted lights above. Why were they blue? Why was everything white or blue?! He felt hatred and terror expanding in his chest like a tumor. He hated hospitals, he hated doctors, why was he here? He would rather die than be here. Why was it so scary? Why did he feel alone? Why was it so quiet? Why was he alone?

Where was the doctor? Where was the nurse? Why were there no toys? Where were the answers!? Maybe he should scream! He felt like screaming, his head hurt, he felt dizzy. Maybe he was dying. Maybe the doctor didn't want to see a dying person. He didn't want to die!

Why him? Why not someone else? What did he do?! Where was his mom?

The room swayed in his vision. *Oh, help. Please help. I'll never do anything bad, but oh, please get me out!* He closed his eyes, breathing quickly. He yearned to go home. The IV shifted inside his arm; he stifled a terrified scream and looked at the swaying IV bag in panic. He was uncontrollably tired and sore. He was cold. Like he was about to freeze to death. He tried to go to sleep but he was too scared.

"Hello?" he said softly.

Nothing.

"Hello!" he called louder.

No response.

He was totally alone. He couldn't imagine himself somewhere else. He was alone and he was scared.

Agramus

Once upon a time, there was a world of magic. Humans, Gnomes, and magical animals alike lived together. No one knew exactly what happened to expel the magic and creatures with magical means from our world, but there are stories passed down of what happened. Some have been altered severely while some are accurate but vague. This story is called 'The Banishment of Necromancy' but is commonly known as 'The Story of Agramus' or just 'Agramus.'

Earth was in its springtime of life, flourishing

underneath the Sun's young petals. Settlements rested upon the rich soil and were shaded by lush trees and berry bushes. The Gnomes lived in a spongy moss forest surrounded by trees that looked like Gnome hats sticking above the ground. Agramus was an hardworking Gnome living with his wife and adopted son. He told stories of rainbows in rivers, of giant roly-polies, and floating islands. He was the joy of the village, so everybody was sorrowed when he and a small group went off to find another place to hunt.

Soon after they left, that's when the Humans came, enslaving the Gnomes and stealing their precious land with weapons the Gnomes had never seen or heard of. The Humans cut down the forest to build themselves houses and fires. Soon moans of pain and despair filled the pungent, smoky air. Endlessly, the Gnomes worked until their hands bled, until they couldn't properly breathe, until they keeled, until they died.

That was when Agramus and his group came back, aghast. The hunters planned the rescue of their people. Quietly they stationed themselves in hiding spots around the village where they observed the Human's strengths and weaknesses. The Humans had better weapons than them, but were easily distracted. They planned. Then they struck. Agramus and a valiant dozen attacked as a distraction while six others evacuated the imprisoned.

Soon Agramus was the only surviving Gnome of the first group and fled into the forest, confusing the Humans with his abrupt escape. Meeting up with the fleeing Gnomes, Agramus searched desperately and found his adopted son, but not his wife, for she died in chains. They marched heavily to the mountains and then climbed to its peak. On top, the Gnomes found a great tree. With no purpose they grabbed the branches and pulled themselves up until they reached the top.

Where they went is lost to time. What happened to the magic and mystical animals? It is said the Humans destroyed every ounce of magic in the world and that, like the Gnomes, the magical animals fled.

That's how the Humans took over the world and how the world lost its magic.

Dream

*With foresight know that this story is written in the weird
fabrications of my mind and delivered while in a state of
unconsciousness. All these people in this story are charming
people that my dream put a dark side to. So be aware of these
facts as you read this utterly baffling short story.*

We were cruising in an open topped car
down a tunnel. The roof was a sky blue,
the floor a blinding artificial green, the
right wall a deep pink, and the left wall a pale rich
orange, all holding a geometric pattern. A kaleido-
scope of Origami butterflies flitted by us in all shades
of purple, while fluffy blue bunnies sat on lawn deco-
rations shaped like deer, and a bright orange lama

stared at us grimly. We laughed until our sides hurt. Leaning over, I stuck out a hand and let it slide along the strange slippery ground with a smile. In the front seat my mom sang songs while my dad told jokes. Beside me, Alexis and Willow—my sisters—played a hand game, and Sawyer read a book. It was bright like it was lit up by hidden lights. Warm as any natural light. Ahead there was a fork in the tunnel, the right side leading to the happy terrain we were in and the other leading into pitch blackness. We cheered happily, leaning eagerly for the strange optical illusions awaiting in the glittering right tunnel. However, once we reached the fork, our bright yellow car stuttered to a stop and let out a wheeze-bang before its light faded and the engine purred itself to sleep.

We simultaneously let out a moan. Perched in front of the dark tunnel my parents argued about what to do. My three siblings had their heads tilted to the ebony darkness. Turning my neck, I froze, startled. Emerging from the dense gloom were three oozing masses. Fat green legs infested with yellow boils propelled the beasties towards us, their midsections pulled sharply into their bodies making their ribs sharply pronounced. Their human-like arms swung to their knees and their heads curled forward like a sloping hill that had been gruesomely attacked. Perched on top of their slimy orange-green heads were fleshy stalks where their glossy eyes roosted. Tattered garments of gray and black hung from their waists to their gooey thighs. A terrifying sight when there is no fast escape.

Willow let out a squeak, calling my parents' attention to her. They froze, then propelled themselves forward to protect us. However, the nightmare animals stopped a few feet away from us. My mom immediately picked up the nerve to ask for gas. When she got no response, she demanded it. Before my mom blew a fuse, my dad interjected and respectively asked if they had gas.

This time they responded. "Yes, but we need ten rubber-bands."

My dad was slightly befuddled and turned to ask my mom if she had any but decided to wait a minute when he saw her face.

"No. I have none," replied my mom, fuming once my dad had nervously asked if she had any rubber-bands on hand. My dad turned to us children. I shrugged, indicating I had none. Sawyer gave my dad a scathing look while Willow said Alexis always hogged the rubber-bands. Alexis opened her mouth to say she had none when she felt something in her pocket and pulled it out. A rubber-band ball. Coughing and embarrassed, she tried to pick out ten rubber-bands. We impatiently waited before Sawyer seized it out of her hands and tossed it to the aliens. Nodding, the leader announced that two had to come with them to collect the gas. Me and Sawyer were immediately volunteered. Dejected, I followed the monsters into the heart of the darkness.

Sawyer complained close behind, babbling. "I don't deserve this! Mom and Dad are the grown-ups. They should be doing this! Not us! Not ME! Or Alexis or Willow! They're super annoying! No surprise you were chosen. But ME! You're annoying, so that totally makes sense." Sawyer ranted excessively.

"Shut up!" I whispered, my face turning bright red.

"No, you shut up," Sawyer said.

My lips complied while my mind made fantasies of punching Sawyer.

"Once we get the gas I'm running and driving the car away, leaving them in the dust." Sawyer muttered.

"I'm getting the gas with you!"

"I'm feeding you to the aliens to escape."

"But I'm helping you!"

"Not right now. You will later."

"Geez." I growled underneath my breath, nearly running into the aliens as we stop.

"Here we are," said the leader, opening a door in thin air. Sawyer and I leaned forward, interested, then the monsters shoved us through the door into a room.

"HEY! LET US OUT!" I shrieked, banging at the door before realizing I'm alone. "SAWYER!" I cried before making myself calm down. Looking around I realized I was in a room made entirely out of windows. Walking cautiously along the narrow wooden frames between the windows I walked to a nearby one and peeked through to see solid concrete near the tip of my nose. I sighed and paused then tried to pull my head out. Stuck. I let out moans of terror and finally yanked my head free, accidentally propelling myself into a large window perched above a city of skyscrapers. Grabbing the frame with my feet I pulled myself upright back into the room of windows. For half an hour, I looked into multiple windows for an escape before coming above a highway with a yellow car in the distance. I waited and timed my jump. Then I hopped into the car next to Sawyer.

"Andrew, turn back, we forgot Elliana," Mom was saying.

"No, she's in the back," Dad said.

"No she isn't."

"Yes she is, Amberlynne."

I filled up my lungs before yelling loudly, "I'm here!"

I hear my dad pause before saying smugly, "See."

"Be quiet," sulked my mom.

"Grand escape, Sawyer," I remarked with a smirk.

"Shut up!" he replies angrily.

I learned that we were visiting some twins. Whether we knew them or not, I haven't a clue. After a blurry time period we drove peacefully around a vacant suburb. Then behind me I heard an evil cackle. Turning, I saw my Uncle Hansen racing towards me, carrying a small bottle of bubblegum pink liquid.

"Go faster!" I yelled at my parents.

"Why?" they replied, slowing down the car. By this time Uncle Hansen had reached the side of the car and was trying to pour the liquid down my throat.

"Because Uncle Hansen's trying to kill me with medicine!" I cried.

Upon hearing this they speed up. As we raced down the road, water crashed into my face. Through the cascade of water I see Mr. Travis trying to drown me with a hose. "Speed up!" I shout, blocking the water from my mouth with my hands.

"No," my mom replies, turning around, smiling like the joker, and wielding a knife. Letting out a high pitched scream, I jumped out of the car and ran from my three pursuers. Racing frantically from Uncle Hansen, Mr. Travis, and my mom, I don't notice the drain until I fell into its murky black depths.

Mist

She stared with incomprehensible horror at the city before her.

The buildings looked blurry and seemed to sway in the gentle breeze, the streets were clogged with cars and people trying to escape the devastation, but no sounds emanated from the beeping horns or screaming mouths. Instead, there was a stifling silence. The skyscraper tops slowly drifted away into gray mist. The people in the streets faded and slowly seemed to unwind like a giant vacuum was sucking them up.

Her purse fell from her cold fingers, hitting the ground with a thud. She watched in grieving terror as Seattle disappeared into nothingness. Her legs gave out beneath her and she clutched her car door, her knees quickly soaked by the wet concrete bridge. She had to be dreaming. The horror beneath her seemed to go in slow-motion making the twenty minutes feel like hours, and then everything was gone. The towering buildings, the people, everything. Her shoulder sockets hurt from awkwardly hanging onto the car and she let her arms fall. Her elbows smacked onto the ground as she looked at the flat bare landscape where Seattle had once sat. Then, with shaking hands, as if waking from a bad dream, she reached into her purse and pulled out her phone to quickly call her mom. The phone buzzed endlessly before her mom's voice instructed to send a voicemail. She called her dad and her brother. Same thing. Tears blurred her sight as she stared at her once upon a time home. She reached up to wipe the tears away. Frowning, she realized her vision was more blurry than before. Once again she raised her fingers to rub them. Then she saw she had none. They ended in blurred stumps. Her hands were quickly fading. She cried silently until she disappeared entirely into mist.

A True Story

Year 2018
Written at age 9

Wind blew the rain against the apartment and into the screen windows, covering the mesh material in small beads of water. The louver windows' glass panes were closed tightly together to keep the rain out. Rain drummed relentlessly against the roof and a chilly breeze wafted through the dining room. Our family of six sat at the dinner table eating in silence, except for the occasional yowls that baby Willow gave as she devoured some dragon fruit. We listened with yearning for the cry of our lost cat. McGonagall had been a gray tabby with large dark eyes and a spirited nature. She was loyal. Had been. She ran away a week before to have her kittens and hadn't returned. We were leaving Indonesia in a few months and couldn't wait for her forever. I was worried. She could have been hit by a car, attacked by a dog, or possibly eaten. Or, as I liked to imagine, purring in some street alley, curled around two orange and one black kitten.

"Meow."

We all jumped up and looked around, startled, then decided we had imagined it. The second time we heard a Meow we leaped from our chairs and opened the screen door.

"McGonagall!" we cried, looking into the rain. All we saw was mossy pavement and the looming car port. Then we heard mad giggling and snorting behind us. Turning around we saw Baby Willow staring at us with her blonde pigtails, and Alexis, my second youngest sister, doubling over in laughter. She had been in a laughing frenzy all week, tricking us into thinking McGonagall had come back. "You jerk! I'm going to steal Orphanee and rip off her head!" I cried. (Orphanee was Alexis' favorite stuffed animal.) My parents glared at Alexis while my older brother,

Sawyer, who had loved the cat the most, looked ready to cry and beat Alexis up at the same time.

"Alexis, if you impersonate the cat again, you are grounded," said my mom with her arms crossed.

Alexis stuck out her bottom lip. "I don't know what impersonate means," Alexis said grumpily.

"It means copy," my dad said.

We sat down again to eat our dinner. Every few minutes I looked at Alexis and stuck my tongue out at her. Later, when we were finishing up the meal, we heard another Meow.

"Alexis!" Me, Sawyer, Dad, and Mom yell. Willow added an undignified screech.

"What?" Alexis says in bewilderment. Just as my parents are about to send Alexis to her room we hear another Meow. Alexis' lips had not moved.

"It wasn't Alexis!" I said in surprise.

We all rushed outside, leaving Willow alone in her high chair. We heard another chorus of meows as we splashed through large puddles.

"McGonagall!" we called into the darkness. My dad turned on his phone's flashlight and we saw a calico kitten. Once it saw us it bolted away into the ditch. My dad chased the kitten wearing socks on his hands. He finally caught the soaking wet creature and brought it into the "no pets allowed" apartment and set it on the kitchen's tile floor, rubbing it dry with his shirt. It meowed sadly. Shaking its colorful coat it stared at us with one blind and one normal eye.

"Can we keep it?" Alexis begged, petting its soggy head.

"It may be someone else's," replied my dad, cuddling it to his chest.

"Let's call it Ginger!" Alexis squealed.

"Let's call it McGonagall 2!" I said loudly.

"We've already had a cat named McGonagall," replied Sawyer, letting the kitten sniff his hand.

"What about we call it Puddles. Because it's rainy outside," advised our mom, petting the kitten.

"Yeah!" we chorused happily.